'We're very disappointed, Jasmin. Your mum and I thought all the extra tuition you've had over the years had sorted that out.'

I was silent. How could I explain that I just didn't seem to be able to remember anything to do with numbers? I didn't understand how they worked and I didn't think I ever would.

'Jasmin, we really think you need to start having on-going maths tuition again,' Mum said gently. 'And for that reason, we want you to leave the Stars at the end of this term.'

For Jacqui

www.thebeautifulgamebooks.co.uk

ORCHARD BOOKS
338 Euston Road, London NW1 3BH
Orchard Books Australia
Level 17/207 Kent Street, Sydney, NSW 2000

First published in 2010 by Orchard Books

A Paperback Original

ISBN 978 1 40830 425 9

A CIP catalogue record for this book is available
from the British Library.

10 9 8 7 6 5 4 3 2 1

Printed in Great Britain

Orchard Books is a division of Hachette Children's Books,
an Hachette UK company.

www.hachette.co.uk

THE BEAUTIFUL GAME

Friends and football – the perfect match

TEAM JASMIN

NARINDER DHAMI

ORCHARD BOOKS

PROLOGUE

Jasmin blinked fiercely to stop the tears in her eyes from falling. She was glad she was the only player left on the pitch after the training session had finished. She didn't want to speak to anyone right at this moment, and she was sure that if any of the other girls said anything to her, she would burst out crying. Jasmin didn't blame Ria, their coach, for the bombshell she'd just dropped on her, though. However much Jasmin didn't want to admit it, she knew only too well that Ria was right...

Reluctantly, Jasmin moved towards the changing-room. All her usual bouncy cheerfulness had vanished as she wondered how on *earth* her life could have changed so quickly in just a short space of time. At the beginning of the new football season, just a few months ago, she'd really been up for it – loving the fact that she had such good friends; enjoying her football and the competition between their team and their biggest rivals, the Belles, to win promotion to the top league; and even *kind* of being pleased to go back to school and move up into year 8. Now all that seemed a million miles away, Jasmin thought unhappily. And it was all because of just *one* person.

She was hoping the others might have already left. But the changing-room door was slightly ajar, and Jasmin could hear her mates' voices as they chatted together and teased each other, occasionally bursting into shrieks of laughter.

Jasmin took a deep breath. She'd have to go into the changing-room now, and tell her friends what had happened. They would be concerned for her, Jasmin knew, but she could only tell them half the story.

They simply *wouldn't* believe the rest...

CHAPTER ONE

If there are eleven girls in a football team, and twenty-two teams in a league, how many footballers is that altogether? That's eleven times twenty-two, which is... Eeek! I have no idea.

'Jasmin! Wake up, you deadhead! She's getting away from you!'

Georgie's thunderous voice from our goalmouth *did* wake me up. I almost jumped out of my skin as one of the Turnwood Tigers midfielders swept past me, the ball at her feet. I'd spent most of the game trying to recite times tables and work out sums in my head, and now I was paying the penalty (football-related joke there, ha ha – no, don't laugh, this is SO not funny).

'I'm there!' I squealed, trying to turn on my heel in a very professional manner to chase after her. But... I'd *noticed* my bootlace was coming undone a little earlier. I'd *meant* to re-tie it. I'd forgotten. Oops.

Now I trod on my trailing lace and almost did myself a severe injury as I stumbled, watching the Tigers player disappear gleefully towards our goal.

'*Jasmin!*' Georgie roared, dancing around in a complete rage. Georgie's very passionate about football and our team, the Springhill Stars (have you noticed?). There's no *way* I'd let her call me a deadhead except when we're on the pitch. If she did it any other time, I'd – well, I'd ask her very politely not to! Georgie can be a *leetle* bit scary sometimes, but she's a sweetie underneath it all, and I love her to bits.

To my relief, I saw Katy run to the rescue. She managed to get a foot between the Tigers player and the ball, and hook it neatly away into touch. Saved by Katy! She's such an *ace* defender, and a great mate, even if she *is* a bit secretive about her family and her home life. But I'm just a nosey parker, any way – curiosity is *so* bad for me!

I heaved another relieved sigh as the ref indicated a Stars' throw-in. The ball must have touched the Tigers player as Katy kicked it out. There wasn't long to go to the end of the game, and we were leading 2-1 thanks to a couple of goals from our brilliant striker, Grace. We were second in our league and we couldn't afford to drop any points, as we were only three behind the leaders, the Blackbridge Belles. We'd done brilliantly the last two games, though, coming back from 2-0 down to draw with the Belles, and also winning our match in the second round of the County Cup 6-0 – YAY! Now, *concentrate*, Jasmin Sharma, I told myself, and stop trying to do maths problems in your head...

'Jasmin, are you OK?' Lauren called as Hannah ran to take the throw-in. 'You look half-asleep!' I *love* Lauren, she's so blonde and petite and pretty and she's a great laugh. Oh, why don't I just save time and tell you that I'm *crazy* about my five best mates on the team – that's Georgie, Katy, Hannah, Lauren and Grace.

'I'm fine,' I yelled back, bending over to tie my bootlace. It wasn't quite true, though. I was thinking about having a good chat with the others when we got changed. Not that there was much they could do to help me, even if they wanted to. But I knew they'd want to, because that's the kind of friends they are.

I get on well with the other girls on the team, but when Grace, Hannah, Lauren, Katy, Georgie and me went on an intensive football course at Easter earlier this year, we *really* bonded, and we've been annoying each other ever since! Ha ha, just joking, we love each other really, but we've had our ups and downs, and *so* much seems to have happened to us. Like I said, I don't know anything about Katy's mysterious home life, but Hannah's had to cope with her evil stepsister, Olivia, moving in with her, and Grace's parents have separated, and Lauren's had problems with her mum and dad working away so much, and Georgie – well, there was BIG trouble when Georgie discovered that her dad was dating our coach, Ria. And as for me...

Well, where do I start? You probably think I'm mad about maths because I've spent the whole match trying to work out sums in my head. Well, go to the bottom of the class and write one hundred lines saying *Jasmin Sharma hates maths!*

It's true. I do hate maths – I'm rubbish at it, that's why I'm practising problems in my head. And it's *so* unfair because my mum and dad are accountants. My oldest sister, Shanti, is training to be an accountant too, and my other sister, Kallie, and my brother, Dan, are going to do the same when they leave school. *Everyone* in my family is a maths genius, except me.

I was doing OK in maths in year 7, but I'm falling behind again now I've gone into year 8. And whenever that's happened in the past, my parents have always arranged private tuition for me. *Nooooo!* I'd rather shave off my lovely, wavy, black hair and be bald than do EXTRA MATHS. Urrrgh!

'To you, Jasmin!' Hannah called as she booted the ball towards me, and, oh boy, was I glad she did, because I was miles away, daydreaming again. I side-footed it to Ruby, one of the other girls on the team, and the three of us, plus Lauren, charged up-field towards Grace who was hovering around the Tigers' goalmouth. Grace had two Tigers defenders watching her every move, because she's the top-scoring striker in our league at the moment (and did I mention that Grace is also tall, blonde, beautiful, kind and caring as well as being a super-fabulous footie player?).

Ruby somehow managed to slot the ball between

the Tigers defenders towards Grace. Grace didn't have much room to manoeuvre in the penalty area, and one of the Tigers defenders tried to clear the ball. She mistimed her kick, though, and the ball flew right up into the air. As it came spinning down into the penalty area again, I was the closest. I leapt forward...

And tripped over my blasted bootlace which had come loose *again* because I hadn't re-tied it properly. But as I staggered, I felt the ball hit me on the backside – of all places! I gave a squeal of surprise, but I was even more shocked when the ball bounced towards Grace's feet. She booted it into the net. Three-one to the Stars!

'Great goal assist, Jasmin' Grace could hardly speak, she was laughing so hard. 'That's the first time I've ever scored with a pass from someone's butt!'

I smiled too, but I was also bright red with embarrassment because *everyone* was laughing – the Stars, our coach Ria and all the parents in the crowd, including my mum. Even the Turnwood Tigers were giggling!

'Typical Jasmin,' Lauren said, giving me a hug as we trotted back into position for kick-off. 'We never know what you're going to do next!'

'And that's why we love you,' Hannah added.

I felt all warm and toasty inside, then, because at least my mates thought I was great, even though I was a maths disaster! I'm dreading the next parents' evening at school, because I just *know* my maths teacher, Miss Platt (great name, huh, *sooo* many opportunities for rude nicknames!) is going to have a serious talk with Mum and Dad about how I'm struggling.

I go to Bramfield Girls', which is a private school, although it isn't as posh as Riverton, where Lauren goes – but then we're not as rich as Lauren's family, either. My parents started up their own accountancy firm recently and it's becoming very successful, but before that they had to scrimp and save to pay school fees for the four of us. So that makes me feel *extra mega-bad* about being so rubbish at maths. It's not like I don't try, but numbers just seem like weird, alien things to me. And, I mean, fractions – what are *they* all about? (Ask someone else if you want to know, because I haven't a clue!)

Don't think I'm a dumbo, though. I get great marks for drama, English and art, but my parents hardly seem to notice...

I was caught up in my own thoughts again, but luckily a few moments later the ref blew her whistle for the end of the game. Immediately Georgie and Katy came racing over from the other end of the pitch to give me a huge bear-hug.

'Great stuff, Jasmin,' Georgie yelled, almost crushing me to death. She doesn't know her own strength, that girl! 'Well done on that clever bum flick!'

'Thank you,' I said modestly, 'I've been practising for *ages*.'

The rest of the team had joined us by this time to celebrate, and they all giggled.

'I'll give you ten quid if you can manage to do that again in the next game, Jas,' Ruby said with a twinkle in her eyes.

'Only ten quid?' I said with a sniff. 'Talent like mine deserves more than that!'

Laughing, we linked arms with each other and headed off the pitch. That's one of the things I *lurve* about the Stars. Grace, Katy, Hannah, Lauren and Georgie are my best mates, but we all get on brilliantly with the other girls – Debs, Alicia, Emily, Jo-Jo and Ruby. We're *really* a team, and it feels so good.

'Fantastic performance, girls.' Our coach, Ria – tall, thin, her beaded dreadlocks tied back in a ponytail – came over to meet us. 'And well done on that very novel goal assist, Jasmin. We must remember to practise that in training.'

The others roared with laughter again as I blushed.

'Did the Belles win too?' Jo-Jo asked anxiously.

We could tell from the look on Ria's face that it wasn't the great news we were hoping for.

'Yes, 2-0,' Ria replied.

'Not again!' Georgie groaned. 'Every time we win, so do they! We need them to lose so we can close that three-point gap.'

'And to do that, *we* need to keep winning,' Ria said calmly. 'Believe me, that's putting pressure on the Belles. We're right behind them, breathing down their necks, and when they slip up, we'll be ready.'

Georgie nodded as we all trooped off to the changing-room. She and Ria had reached some sort of uneasy truce, and Georgie was OK with her as our coach now. But she still didn't like Ria dating her dad. I often wondered what would happen if Ria and Mr Taylor decided to get married, but I hadn't had a chance to discuss this with Georgie yet. (OK, maybe it's just because I'm too scared!)

The changing-room was busy and noisy, as the Stars Under-Tens and Under-Twelves teams were also playing at home today. We bagged our favourite corner and began to strip off our kits.

'So what's with you today, Jasmin?' Lauren asked, pulling her shirt off. 'You looked like you were a million miles away.'

'I was,' I sighed.

'Why?' Katy enquired as she brushed out her long silky dark hair.

'I was trying to work out sums in my head, and failing miserably,' I groaned.

'Trouble with maths again?' Hannah said sympathetically.

I nodded. 'I've told you before that I don't think my mum and dad realise how stupid I am at maths,' I confided. I wriggled out of my shorts and drop-kicked them into my bag. 'They just think I'm a bit dippy and I don't concentrate, because that's what my teachers at primary school used to say about me. They don't realise I concentrate *so* hard in my maths class that my brain nearly explodes out of both my ears!'

'Lovely,' Grace said with a grin. 'You should talk to them about it.'

'They won't listen.' I pulled my shirt off. 'They'll

just think I need to try harder, and that means they'll arrange extra tuition for me until I catch up again. That's what they've always done before.' I heaved a glum sigh. 'Last time, when I was in year 6, they were thinking about keeping Mrs Rehman, the maths tutor, on when I moved to Bramfield, but I managed to talk them out of it. Just.'

'Gross!' Georgie exclaimed. 'I hate maths too.'

'Double gross,' I agreed. 'But the next parents' evening isn't till February, so maybe I can catch up on my own before then.'

'I like maths,' Hannah remarked, as she tied up her chestnut-coloured hair in a ponytail.

'You're unnatural,' Georgie said, giving her a good-natured poke.

'Right, all mention of maths is banned for the rest of the weekend,' I announced. 'You're all still coming to our Diwali party tonight, aren't you?'

'Of course,' Katy replied. 'I'm *dying* to wear that pink shalwaar kameez you lent me.'

'You can wear your own clothes if you like,' I offered.

'No, we're all dressing up Indian-style, even Georgie,' Lauren said, eyeballing her to make sure she agreed. Georgie groaned, but didn't say anything.

She's not a girlie girl, our Georgie, and it's a real struggle to get her to wear anything that isn't a Spurs shirt and trackie bottoms – although she's been a bit better since we gave her a make-over not long ago. She even knows how to apply lip-gloss now!

The six of us grabbed our bags and headed out of the changing-room together, yelling goodbye to the rest of the team.

'So, do you get presents at Diwali?' Katy asked curiously.

I nodded. 'I get money, mostly.'

'But you celebrate Christmas too, don't you, Jasmin?' Grace said.

'Yep, some Hindus don't, but *we* do,' I explained. 'So that means in about six weeks' time, I'll get another lot of presents on Christmas Day, tee hee, yay for me!'

'Sounds like a brilliant scam!' Georgie remarked as we walked out into the car park. 'See you tonight then, guys.'

There was a chorus of goodbyes. Katy slipped out of the gates on her own after refusing offers of a lift from Hannah and Lauren. Georgie and Hannah went off together to Hannah's mum's car, and Lauren skipped over to her dad's monster Mercedes.

Meanwhile, Grace's father was waiting for her at the far end of the car park. Grace's parents separated last month, although they hadn't decided yet whether to divorce or not. But I knew that Grace was gutted, and also that she and her twin sister Gemma were secretly hoping that their mum and dad would get back together again.

'Hi, Mum.' I strolled over to my mum's little old red banger and jumped in.

'Hello, darling.' Mum started up the engine as I belted myself up (sounds painful!). 'You certainly created a bit of a stir today.'

I grinned. 'I did, didn't I?'

As we drove home, we talked about the match for a bit, and then Mum started fretting about how much work she still had to do for the Diwali party.

'Are all the girls coming tonight?' Mum asked.

'Yes, I can't wait!' I replied happily.

'By the way,' Mum said as they stopped at a red light, 'I meant to tell you, I've invited Mrs Horowitz.'

I could hardly believe my ears 'What!' I yelled. 'You've invited *Mrs Horowitz* to our Diwali party?' Mrs Horowitz was the head of maths at my school, and she was a real scary Mary! Everyone was terrified of her, even the other maths teachers. 'Why? You and Dad don't even know her!'

I had a horrible suspicion that maybe Mum and Dad had already realised that I was struggling with maths, and *that* was why they'd invited Mrs Horowitz: for a council of war...

'Your dad and I have invited some of our clients to the party,' Mum explained. 'Mrs Horowitz's husband is an architect, and our firm have just taken over his accounts.' She drew up behind a smart silver car parked outside our house. 'It's not a problem, is it, Jasmin?'

'No,' I mumbled. I would just have to hope that the Horror Witch – that's what we call her! – didn't decide to have a chat with Mum and Dad about my maths. But why would she? It was supposed to be a party, after all, not a parents' evening.

Suddenly the front door of our house flew wide open. Dad charged out, followed by Shanti and Kallie. Bringing up the rear was Dan, who looked like he'd just rolled out of bed as he was barefoot and trying to pull a T-shirt over his head.

'Surprise!' Dad proclaimed, dangling a set of keys inches from Mum's nose.

'Keys,' Mum said drily. 'Just what I always wanted. What's going on?'

'Well, if you don't *want* a brand-new car...' Dad said with a shrug and he pointed at the posh silver car parked outside our house.

Mum's mouth fell open in disbelief. The rest of us began clapping and cheering as Dad unlocked the driver's door.

'Did you know about this?' I whispered to Kallie.

She shook her head. 'We only found out about half an hour ago when the car arrived.'

'Raj, we can't afford it—' Mum began as Dad hustled her into the driver's seat.

'Of course we can,' Dad replied, handing her the keys. 'Business is booming. I *knew* we were right to set up on our own.'

'You shouldn't have,' Mum gasped, her eyes shining. 'But thank you!'

Dad turned to us. 'I can see it now,' he said triumphantly. 'We can build this into a *real* family firm, with all of us working together when the four of you have done your accountancy training. In a few years time, we'll be millionaires!'

Shanti, Dan and Kallie laughed, but not me. I was staring at Dad in horror. What did he mean? *I* didn't want to be an accountant!

'Right, let's take this new baby for a spin,'

Dad said, trying to close the driver's door, but Mum resisted.

'No, Raj, I've got loads to do before the party tonight—' she began.

'Ah, come on, just a quick one,' Dad wheedled. 'The kids can carry on without us.'

'Well, OK,' Mum agreed reluctantly. 'Shanti, can you take your dad's car and go and pick up the food I ordered from the take-away, please? Dan, get the fairy-lights up around the front door and—'

'Just *go*, Mum,' Shanti said, closing the door. We all watched as Mum started up the engine and then, with a few bunny hops, set off cautiously down the road.

'C'mon, guys, let's get to it,' Shanti went on, heading back towards the house with Kallie.

I hung back with Dan, who still looked half-asleep as he ambled back up the front path.

'Do you think Dad *really* meant that?' I asked him. 'About us *all* joining the family firm?'

'Sure, why not?' Dan yawned hugely. 'Beats working for someone else, doesn't it? What's the matter, Jammy Dodger?' He slung his arm around my shoulder and gave me a squeeze. 'Don't you love us any more?'

(Can I just explain that when I was a tiny tot, I couldn't say my name very well when I was learning to talk, and I kept calling myself *Jamsin* instead of *Jasmin*, and that got shortened to *Jammy* and then, occasionally, I also get called *Jammy Dodger*. It's all extremely embarrassing.)

'That's not the point, idiot brother,' I replied. 'I just didn't realise Dad was expecting us kids to join the family business, that's all.'

'Well, that's partly why he set it up, I think,' Dan said with a shrug. 'It doesn't mean we have to join straight away, you know. We can still go to uni, go travelling, whatever.'

'Yes,' I said in a small voice. With a sickening feeling, I realised that my future was being all mapped out by my parents. Leave school, go to college, become an accountant...

My mind was clouded with anxiety. Maybe I was stupid to worry about the future. After all, I was only twelve, thirteen just after Christmas. *Anything* could happen in the next few years before I had to make some career decisions. But now I was beginning to feel that those decisions were being taken out of my hands.

And there was one thing I knew for sure: I definitely

did NOT want to be an accountant.

Which meant there was big trouble ahead...

'Well, look at you!' I said admiringly, as Grace and Hannah posed on our doorstep like models. They'd arrived for our Diwali party wearing the Indian suits I'd lent them – Hannah's was emerald green with crystal embroidery, and Grace's was pale blue and gold (I'd had to borrow them both from Kallie, as Hannah and Grace are both a bit taller than me). Both girls had put their hair up for the occasion, and they looked *stunning*.

'And what about *you*?' Grace laughed. 'You look like a Bollywood film star!'

I was wearing an outfit I'd had for my aunt's wedding – a long turquoise skirt, or *lengha* as we call it, and a matching *choli*, which is a little fitted top, all embroidered with glittery peacock feathers.

'Loving the fairy-lights around the front door,' Hannah commented as they came in, followed by Hannah's parents and Mr Kennedy, Grace's dad. The party had just started, and guests were arriving every few minutes.

'Dan spent all afternoon putting lights up around

the house,' I told her. 'He fell off the stepladder twice and almost electrocuted himself, I think!'

'Well, it was worth it,' Hannah said with a grin. 'Diwali *is* the Festival of Lights, after all. It looks gorgeous, Jasmin.'

The dining room door at the end of the hall was open and we could see right through to the conservatory at the back of the house. There were fairy-lights strung everywhere, and Shanti and Mum had put candles in tall glass lanterns on the window ledges. With the house lights dimmed, it all looked magical. Bollywood music was playing, and people were already milling around carrying drinks and plates of curry, rice, naan bread and samosas.

'Thanks for coming,' I said to the Fleetwoods and Grace's dad, as the doorbell rang again. 'There's loads of food and drink in the dining room.'

'Great, I'm starving!' Mr Kennedy exclaimed.

'I asked my mum to come too, but she wasn't keen when she knew Dad was invited,' Grace confided as Hannah went to open the front door.

'Oh, I'm *so* sorry, Grace,' I said, patting her arm. We all had problems, I guess. I was *dying* to talk more to my mates about all this maths stuff that was going on with my parents, but not tonight. I just wanted to enjoy the party. We usually got together on Sundays, even if it was just for an hour or two, but we weren't meeting up tomorrow because Lauren and Georgie had family stuff going on. And Mum had already told me that I'd be spending the day helping to clear up after the party (thanks, Mum!).

None of the other girls were at my school, which meant we wouldn't all be together again until training on Tuesday. So my problems would have to wait until then. But at least Grace had reminded me that I wasn't the only one with family hassles, I thought, glancing at her downcast face.

Hannah opened the door to Katy, who looked lovely in my pink shalwaar kameez, with her black hair in a high ponytail. Just as Hannah was closing the door behind her, we heard someone running up the path, and there was Georgie. We all burst into spontaneous cheers when we saw that she was wearing the navy blue and white silk Indian suit I'd borrowed from Kallie.

'Thanks, you lot,' Georgie said with a bow. 'But don't get overexcited, I'm only wearing it because it's Spurs colours, ha ha.'

'Ooh, I spy make-up!' I declared, peering at

Georgie's face. 'Any flying pigs out there, girls? Or a blue moon?'

'How did you get here, Georgie?' Hannah asked.

'My dad and Ria brought me,' Georgie said, a touch grumpily.

I glanced out of the front door and saw Mr Taylor, Georgie's dad, and Ria come in through the garden gate. Ria looked totally gorgeous in a black satin dress and killer red patent heels.

'God, Ria looks *fabulous*,' I began, but stopped abruptly as Grace stepped very slightly on my toes. 'Um – let's go and grab some food, shall we, girls?' I said quickly. 'Once my relatives get scoffing, there'll be nothing left!'

Leaving my mum to greet Ria and Georgie's dad, I led the way down the hall through the crowd and into the dining room. There we joined the scrum for the buffet.

'Jasmin, there's enough food here to feed the whole street,' Georgie declared, cheering up visibly as she spotted the curries, rice, naan bread and samosas.

I was just handing round some plates when Lauren breezed into the room, her good-looking, glamorous mum and dad behind her.

'Oh, trust you guys to start the feast without me!'

Lauren teased. 'I'm glad I got here before Georgie ate the lot.'

'Hilarious,' Georgie commented, spooning a whole load of potato and pea curry onto her plate. 'Us goalies need to keep our strength up, you know.'

The Fleetwoods, Mr Kennedy, Mr Taylor, Ria and Lauren's parents were all chatting away happily together, so we left them to it.

'Jasmin, are there any more samosas?' Hannah wailed as a large auntie in a bright green sari sailed in front of us, grabbed the last three samosas and bore them away in triumph.

'Sure, there are another two thousand in the kitchen!' I replied. 'Why don't you lot go and bag some seats in the conservatory, and I'll get us a plateful.'

I wove my way through the crowd towards the kitchen, where Dan had congregated with a gang of his mates, all clutching bottles of beer. Having loaded up a plate with a teetering tower of samosas, I was about to head off into the dining room and through to the conservatory when I suddenly spotted MRS HOROWITZ! My mum was escorting her into the dining room, along with a man in a dark suit who must have been her architect husband.

'Oh no!' I groaned under my breath. I didn't want to ruin what had been a fun evening up till now by having to be polite to the Horror Witch. So I turned and headed out of the opposite door. I'd have go the long way round through the living room to reach the conservatory, but it was worth it!

'Ah, Jasmin, there you are.' Another auntie stopped me in my tracks in the doorway and pinched a samosa from my plate. 'How are you, sweetie?'

'Fine, Auntie,' I squeaked, casting an anxious glance over my shoulder in case Mum was leading the Horowitzes towards the kitchen. There they were, coming in through the other door!

Luckily someone tapped Auntie on the shoulder then to say hello. I seized my opportunity and legged it, my plate of samosas in one hand and holding up my lengha with the other. It was like a movie – *Escape from the Horror Witch!*

'What's up, Jasmin?' Katy asked as I joined the girls on one of the big cream sofas in the conservatory. I was relieved they'd chosen to sit there, as we were partially hidden behind a wicker screen and some tall palms in pots. 'You look a bit flustered.'

'Oh, I'm fine,' I replied, handing round the samosas. I wasn't going to spoil the party by moaning about Mrs Horowitz and my maths problems right now.

'So, what about the matches up till Christmas, then?' Lauren said, taking a gulp of Coke. 'Do you think any of the teams who are playing the Belles will manage to beat them, and give us a chance to close that three-point gap?'

So we got stuck into a long conversation, then, giving our opinions, and – yes! – arguing with each other about this team and the other, but it was all good fun, really. Then Lauren asked me to show them a few Bollywood moves, so we had a dance around the sofa and it was a huge laugh. Even Georgie joined in, although she was about as graceful as a baby elephant with a limp (her words, not mine!). I was having such a fun time, I even got brave and offered to go and fetch us another round of Cokes. And that's when I heard what I heard...

Our conservatory is really big and runs the whole length of the house, so there were lots of people in there. It was also quite dimly lit, so at first I didn't see Mum and Mrs Horowitz perched on a window seat behind a display of plants. I *did* hear them, though.

'Well, that's very disappointing,' Mum was saying. 'We were hoping that Jasmin would have learnt to apply herself better by now.'

Oh, you know how it is. I *wasn't* going to listen, but when I heard my name I couldn't help it...

'She's had problems with maths in the past,' Mum went on, 'but we think it's only because she has trouble concentrating in class properly. All her subject teachers have said before that she's far too easily distracted.'

No, it isn't, Mum! I thought. *It's because I just don't like maths and I'm no good at it.*

'Mmm...' The Horror Witch sounded less convinced. 'Well, I just thought I'd let you know that Jasmin's teacher, Miss Platt, has mentioned her concerns to me.'

'Thank you,' Mum replied gratefully. 'I shall have to discuss this with my husband, but we can certainly get her a maths tutor again.'

No!

'And maybe we'll have to look at cutting some of Jasmin's extra-curricular activities too, to make more time for studying,' Mum added. 'She goes to the art club at school, and she's just joined the drama group so she'll be helping with the Christmas pantomime. And then, of course, there's her football...'

CHAPTER TWO

'God, that maths homework was tough,' my friend Izzie Greene moaned as we headed into school on Monday morning. 'I almost fried my brain doing those fractions over the weekend.'

'Did you get yours done, Jasmin?' asked my other mate, May Pang.

I shook my head. 'Not yet. It doesn't have to be in till Wednesday, does it?'

'No, but it doesn't get any better if you put it off,' Izzie warned with a sigh, flicking back her long red hair. 'I swear, those improper fractions gave me nightmares last night.'

'I love that name *improper fractions*,' May remarked as we wove our way through the crowds of gossiping girls to hang up our coats. 'It sounds like they're going to do something bad like fart in class or something.'

Izzie and I laughed. I *knew* I shouldn't put off my maths homework, because I'd be panicking like mad when I finally got around to it. But I'd had too much going on over the weekend to think about fractions.

On Sunday morning after the party, my mum and dad had said they wanted to have a quick chat with me. I'd been so nervous my hair had almost been standing on end! I hadn't heard any more of the conversation between Mum and Mrs Horowitz at the party because one of my uncles had come up to talk to me just then (and to ask me how I was getting on with my maths, obviously – my family are maths-mad!).

I thought maybe Mum and Dad were going to tell me something really drastic, like the Horror Witch had suggested I give up football and everything else I really enjoyed, and spend my whole time doing MATHS.

It hadn't been *quite* that terrifying. But it was bad enough.

'And so Mrs Horowitz mentioned that she and Miss Platt thought you were having a few problems in your maths classes,' Mum had explained. Which I already knew because, of course, I'd been eavesdropping.

'We've decided that you need a maths tutor again, Jasmin,' Dad said. 'The trouble is, we're not quite sure how you're going to fit in extra tuition with all the other stuff you do. So—'

DANGER!

'Look, Dad, I'll be fine,' I broke in before he could say *anything* about giving up football or anything else. 'I'll really get my head down before Christmas and sort myself out. There's nothing to worry about.'

My parents looked doubtful.

'And if I need any extra help, I can ask you, Kallie, Dan or Shanti,' I added. I'd done that in the past, but it *never* worked because they were all so much better at maths than me, I could never understand the explanation, never mind the answer! But I was so desperate, I'd try *anything*.

'Well, as we're all so busy with Christmas coming up and business booming, maybe we'll wait for a month or two,' Dad said at last. I was careful not to breathe a huge sigh of relief. 'But we'll definitely sort out some tuition for you over the Christmas holidays, and maybe after that too.'

Great Christmas present, huh?

'And we expect to see you doing better in class before then, Jasmin.' Mum wagged her finger at me teasingly, but I knew she meant what she was saying. 'We know you have the ability, but you've always been a bit dreamy and head-in-the-clouds, sweetie, haven't you?'

I nodded dutifully. That was how the rest of my family saw me: as the dippy, ditsy little kid who was the odd one out. Oh, don't get me wrong, I'm not saying they don't love me – 'cos I know they *do* – but they can't seem to get their heads around the fact that I'm just not exactly the same as *them*.

So I was kind of saved – for the moment, anyway. But that left me with a whole new problem. How the hell was I going to improve my maths *and* keep on doing the things I loved like football, drama and art? And *especially* football, because of the other girls. I couldn't imagine my life now without Grace, Hannah, Lauren, Georgie and Katy. But something would have to give time-wise if I had maths tuition every week, and I was guessing, with a cold feeling of dread, that it would be football. It took up a lot of time because we trained Tuesday and Thursday evenings and had a match every Saturday morning...

I followed Izzie and May into our classroom. Bramfield's an old Victorian school with lots of modern extensions, but our classroom is in one of the oldest parts of the building. It's got a tiled fireplace and a high ceiling with beautiful plaster decorations all over it. The room's chilly in winter and boiling in summer, but I love it. I sometimes wished I went to Greenwood High, where Hannah, Grace, Katy and Georgie go. It sounds like they have a great laugh at school, and Lauren and I miss out on all of that...

Suddenly Izzie elbowed me violently in the ribs.

'Ow,' I complained. 'That hurt.'

'Look,' Izzie whispered, jerking her head at the open door.

Our form teacher, Mrs Myers, was bustling into the classroom, register in hand. Mrs Myers is a sweetie, but she *does* remind me of a hen! She's short and round with red hair and she always scuttles everywhere very fast – oh, and she even *sounds* a bit like a hen, clucking away crossly when she tells you off.

Behind Mrs Myers was a girl none of us had ever seen before. She was tall and slender and she had long, very blonde and very shiny hair, which was piled up on top of her head and held in place with a couple of red barrettes. But what *really* made you stare at her were her eyes. They were very large and the bluest blue I'd ever seen, with thick, sooty lashes.

'Who's *she*?' I murmured to Izzie and May as the girl followed Mrs Myers into the room. She was staring around, looking completely confident and self-possessed. I was fascinated to see that the boring blue and white Bramfield uniform looked like a designer outfit the way this girl wore it. Her navy skirt seemed to fit and flare much better than ours did, and it showed off her long legs in over-the-knee matching socks. Her shoes looked incredibly cool and expensive with cone-shaped heels and ankle straps (the kind of shoes which were *definitely* not allowed).

'Must be a new girl,' May whispered as Mrs Myers waited for silence. 'But it's a funny time to start in the middle of the autumn term.'

'Girls, this is Sienna Gerard,' Mrs Myers

announced. 'I hope you'll all help her settle in quickly.' Her eyes roamed around the room and finally fixed on me, Izzie and May. 'I'm sure you three will look after our new girl,' Mrs Myers clucked briskly. 'Sienna, you can go and sit with Jasmin, May and Izzie.'

'Thank you, Mrs Myers,' Sienna drawled. She had a soft, husky voice and a slight American accent.

I felt ridiculously excited as Sienna strolled over to our table, as if we were going to be sitting with a celebrity or something!

'Hi there,' Sienna said briefly, taking the empty chair.

'Hi,' Izzie, May and I chorused. We all sounded breathless with excitement, as if we'd just been introduced to the Queen! I was *dying* to ask Sienna where she'd come from and why she'd started school in the middle of a term, but we had to keep quiet while Mrs Myers took the register.

'Right, girls, ten minutes of *silent* reading before assembly,' Mrs Myers announced. Everyone began searching for their books, and that gave me a chance to say something.

'Are you American, Sienna?' I asked quietly, bursting with curiosity.

Sienna shook her head. 'Hey, I know I have a bit of an accent, right?' she said with a stunning smile that showed off perfect white teeth. 'But I was born in England. We lived in the States for the last three years because of my dad's job. We were in Australia before that, and Malaysia and Hong Kong before *that*.'

'Cool,' Izzie gasped, her eyes wide.

'Why are you back here, then?' asked May.

'Oh, my dad just got offered some mega-bucks promotion out of the blue,' Sienna replied, shrugging her shoulders elegantly. 'So we came home.'

'Where do you live?' I wanted to know.

'In the countryside, just outside Melfield.' Sienna turned her *amazing* eyes to look at me. They were so blue, I almost felt hypnotised by them. 'My parents bought Eastfields Manor. Do you know it?'

I nodded, trying not to look *seriously* impressed. Everyone in Melfield knew Eastfields Manor – it was a huge, palatial Georgian manor house standing in acres of grounds. The Gerards must be *loaded*. I glanced at May and Izzie who were staring at Sienna in fascination.

'Didn't your parents want you to go to Riverton?' I asked a bit nosily. Bramfield was a really good school, but Riverton, where Lauren was a student, was extra-special and extra-expensive. But it sounded like the Gerards could afford it.

'I wanted to choose for myself,' Sienna said calmly. 'And *I* decided on Bramfield.'

I was now even *more* impressed. I could just imagine my parents' faces if I told them I wanted to choose my own school! But then, Sienna seemed so grown-up and sure of herself, maybe her parents respected her opinion. *Which is more than my parents do,* I thought gloomily, as I remembered my future career as –YUK! – an accountant.

We couldn't say anything more because everyone else was reading, and Mrs Myers was glaring pointedly at us. I opened my book, but I couldn't help sneaking the occasional look at Sienna. While the rest of us were reading stuff we were studying in English lit, she'd pulled a celebrity mag out of her bag!

I could already see that having Sienna around was going to liven up boring old school no end! And at least it would take my mind off M-A-T-H-S...

'Come on, Jasmin,' Ria called. 'Get in there and fight for the ball!'

'I'm trying!' I squealed. We were finishing off our Tuesday night training session with a practice game and I lunged forward, trying to get the ball away from Lauren, who was on the opposing team. But my foot slipped, and I ended up almost doing the splits as Lauren easily avoided me!

'Get with the programme, Jasmin!' Georgie yelled from our goal. 'This is a football game, not a dance class!'

I chased after Lauren and just managed to intercept the ball as she tried to pass to Alicia. Then I chipped it to Grace – probably the best move I'd made all night! Grace caught the ball on the volley and smashed it into the back of the other team's net.

'Good stuff, Jasmin,' said Ria with a smile. 'Can we see a lot more like that, please?'

'I'll try,' I panted as the session ended. My mind just *hadn't* been on football tonight. I still hadn't had a chance to fill the girls in yet on what had been happening with my parents, and I couldn't wait to talk it through with them. And then there were all those nasty little fractions waiting for me when I got home!

'You've been looking a bit out of it tonight, Jas,' Lauren observed as we trooped off the pitch at the end of training.

'Yes, I noticed that too,' Hannah said. 'Fab party on Saturday, by the way.'

'Thanks,' I sighed. 'But there's a *lot* I haven't told you.'

'I knew it!' Grace exclaimed. 'You just haven't been yourself tonight.'

'Yes, you haven't got that naughty Jasmin twinkle in your eyes,' Hannah agreed.

'Come on, tell us,' Georgie urged.

So I told them about Dad saying all that stuff about us kids joining the family firm, and I also related the conversation I'd overheard between Mum and Mrs Horowitz at the party. Then I told them what my parents had said to me on Sunday morning about having extra tuition. By the time I'd finished, their mouths were hanging open in shock.

'God, that's the *pits*!' Georgie declared as we went into the changing-room. 'Jasmin, you *can't* leave the Stars. It just wouldn't be the same without you.'

'I know we've said this before, but couldn't you just tell your parents that you don't like maths and you don't want to be an accountant?' Katy suggested gently.

'I've tried,' I said with a heartfelt sigh. 'But, you know, when we were growing up my mum didn't work, and so it was a real struggle for them to send us all to private school. They sacrificed a lot for that. And I'd feel so *bad* telling them I don't want to join the family firm. They're so proud of it now it's a big success.'

'But, Jasmin, this is your future we're talking about,' Lauren pointed out.

'Tell me about it,' I sighed. 'But I'm just going to have to put my head down and try to get the Horror Witch and my maths teacher Miss Platt off my back.'

Grace slid her arm around me and gave me a sympathetic squeeze. 'I wish we could do something to help.'

'Maybe we can,' Hannah said.

We all looked at her in surprise.

'*I* could give you some maths coaching, Jasmin,' Hannah went on, smiling at me.

I stared at her.

'Would you?' I asked hopefully. 'That would be *fantastic*!'

'No problem,' Hannah replied. 'Have you got any maths homework right now?'

I pulled a face. 'Yes, and it's got to be handed in tomorrow. EEK!'

'OK, I'll call you when I get home and give you a hand,' Hannah suggested.

'Sorted!' Georgie declared enthusiastically, opening her locker. 'And we can all try to help, as well as Hannah. Although I'm not much better at maths than you are, Jasmin!'

'Yep, we've *got* to keep Jasmin in the Stars, where she belongs,' Lauren agreed.

See? I *told* you my fab mates wouldn't let me down!

A few hours later I was mooching around my bedroom, waiting for Hannah's call. My room was a mess, as usual, but it was *my* mess and I felt comfy in it. I always had piles of books and DVDs lying around, and on one wall I pinned up my artwork from school. In a corner was the big cage where my chinchilla, Ludmilla, was fast asleep. Georgie, Hannah, Katy, Grace and Lauren had thought it was *hilarious* when I told them that I had a chinchilla for a pet, but now they all adore Ludmilla nearly as much as I do! She is *so* cute with her big round dark eyes and thick, deep grey fur, just like expensive velvet.

I was feeling loads better about doing those awful fractions now! But I couldn't help wondering how

Hannah was going to succeed in making me understand maths, when countless teachers had tried and failed!

Suddenly my phone rang.

'Hi, Jasmin,' Hannah said cheerfully. 'Are you OK to talk?'

'Yep, I'm in my bedroom on my own.'

'Me too.' Hannah heaved a sigh. 'Olivia's downstairs having a row with Dad so I *had* to get away. He doesn't like Olivia's new boyfriend, Freddie.'

'Why not?'

'I'm not sure,' Hannah replied. 'But I think it *might* be something to do with the fact that Freddie bunks off school regularly and has a tattoo of a spider's web on his neck. Other than that, he seems quite pleasant.'

I had to laugh. When Hannah first joined the Stars, we thought she was really quiet because she didn't say much, but she's got a great sense of humour, and some of the things she says just crack us up.

'I don't think Olivia really likes him any way,' Hannah went on. 'She just wants to wind Dad up. Shall we start your homework?'

'Sure,' I agreed reluctantly. I would have liked just

to stay chatting to Hannah for a bit longer. I had lots to tell her about Sienna, who had turned out to be even *more* thrilling than I could have imagined. Izzie, May and I had got to know her better during the last couple of days, and Sienna had been everywhere and done everything. She'd ridden elephants in India, shopped in Hong Kong, skied in Switzerland, sunbathed in Florida, lived in Los Angeles, and done anything else exotic and wonderful you can think of.

But any way, back to fractions. Proper and improper!

'What's your first sum?' asked Hannah.

'Five tenths divided by two tenths,' I groaned.

'Tell me what do you *think* the answer is?' Hannah urged.

I stared at the numbers. I knew we'd done this in class with Miss Platt, but I simply couldn't remember how to work it out. I took a guess.

'Er – three tenths?' I said hesitantly.

'No, that's subtraction!' Hannah pointed out. 'When you're dividing fractions, you have to switch the second set of fractions around and then multiply them, to begin with—'

'Ooh, *now* I remember!' I sighed with frustration. 'But it's so confusing, trying to remember to multiply when there's a division sign in the sum.'

'Maybe it'd be easier to do this on MSN,' Hannah suggested. 'You work out each sum and send it to me, and I'll tell you if it's right or not.'

Even though Hannah had given me a clue how to do the first sum, I still came up with the wrong answer – three, when it should have been two and a half. Then, slowly we went through the rest of my homework. I *kind* of understood it a little better as Hannah explained the process over and over again, but I knew it would go right out of my head as soon as I went to sleep!

Anyway, it was taking so long that in the end, Hannah just *told* me some of the answers. I knew it was cheating a bit and I felt *really* bad about it, but I just didn't have a choice. Otherwise I'd have to give up all the things I enjoyed most, including football. So what else could I do?

What would *you* do?

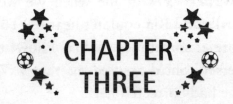

CHAPTER THREE

'Jasmin, I don't know what to say,' Miss Platt declared, handing me back my maths homework. It was covered with red ticks! 'For the last two weeks, you've been steadily improving, and shown what you can do when you *concentrate*. Well done.'

'Thank you, Miss,' I mumbled. I was relieved, but I also felt like a right phoney. It was Friday, ten days after that Tuesday last week when Hannah helped me with my fractions. And since then, Hannah had been doing more and more of my homework for me...

'I shall tell Mrs Horowitz how pleased I am with

you,' Miss Platt went on, looking thrilled. How sad is that? I think teachers must lead very boring lives!

Hannah had been helping me out almost every night by phone, email and MSN, and also at the training sessions on Tuesdays and Thursdays. So had the others. Georgie would do things like whisper *What's 7x7?* at me when we were doing training drills and Ria couldn't hear us. The trouble was, Georgie sometimes didn't know the right answer herself. She'd assured me that 7x7 was 48, until Grace had corrected her!

We'd had a match the previous Saturday against Melfield United, which we'd won easily, 2-0. The Belles had won again too, though, which was a pain because it meant the points gap between us was still the same. Anyway, on the Sunday we'd met up at Lauren's house, and – listen to this – the girls had prepared a whole series of maths questions for me, based on our league table!

'So if we win our next two games, and the Belles lose one of theirs and draw the other, how many points will there be between us *then*?' Grace had fired at me.

'Our goal difference is a bit worse than the Belles,' Katy had chimed in. 'How many do we need to score to make it better than theirs?'

'If there are twenty teams in our league, how many players is that altogether?' Hannah wanted to know.

Honestly, my head was spinning with numbers. I swear I'd had a nightmare last night where I was chased down the road by a huge number five with legs! I was *so* grateful to the girls for all their help, even though coping with my maths classes was still a bit difficult. Because I was "improving", Miss Platt was beginning to expect me to put my hand up and answer questions all the time – *help!*

'Now, Sienna...' Miss Platt glanced over at Sienna who was sitting with me, Izzie and May. We'd become quite good mates since she'd arrived, and to our amazement and delight, Sienna seemed to like hanging around with the three of us. I'd secretly thought that, being so gorgeous and cool and confident, she might want to hook up with Melissa Grey and her gang (also known as the Prom Queens or Wannabe WAGs because they *so* think they're all that!). But Sienna didn't seem interested in them. I was enormously flattered that she preferred to be mates with us, and I knew that May and Izzie were too.

'I haven't had any homework from you, Sienna,' Miss Platt went on, raising an enquiring eyebrow.

'No, Miss Platt,' Sienna replied calmly. 'The dog ate it.'

There was stunned silence, and then a few people giggled nervously.

'I *beg* your pardon?' Miss Platt spluttered.

'Our dog, Chanel, ate my maths homework,' Sienna repeated. 'She's a Bichon Frise, and they're quite naughty dogs, you know.'

Miss Platt's eyes almost popped out of her head. I glanced at Sienna and was astounded to see how cool she looked. I'd never actually *heard* anyone use that joke excuse – *The dog ate my homework* – before! Was Sienna lying? Looking at her smooth, innocent face, I simply couldn't tell.

'I'll do it again tonight and bring it tomorrow,' Sienna added.

'I think that would be a very good idea,' Miss Platt replied, still looking somewhat flustered. 'And I suggest you also bring a note from your mother confirming that your dog – er – ate your homework.'

'No problem,' Sienna said. Her ever-so-slightly bored tone implied that her mother would write whatever Sienna asked her to, whether it was true or not.

As Miss Platt handed Izzie her homework, I sneaked another glance at Sienna. She didn't seem to care one bit about getting told off. Part of the reason why she was so fascinating, I thought, was that you were never quite sure what she was going to do next...

'Miss Platt.' Sienna raised her hand languidly. 'May I leave the room, please? I feel sick.'

Miss Platt stared suspiciously at her. 'Is that true, Sienna?'

'Yes, Miss,' Sienna said weakly. Suddenly her shoulders began to heave and she retched loudly, putting her hand to her mouth. If Sienna *was* pretending, she was doing *the* best impression of someone about to spew!

'Go straight to the school office and see the nurse,' Miss Platt ordered her nervously. Sienna rushed out, her hand over her mouth. The other girls in the class started murmuring to each other, and Izzie and May stared at me with big, excited eyes.

'Do you think Sienna really *is* sick?' May whispered as Miss Platt attempted to quieten everyone down.

'I don't know,' I said with a shrug. It seemed impossible to guess when Sienna was lying or when she was telling the truth. I envied her that supreme self-confidence she seemed to have.

The rest of maths class dragged on, but at last the bell sounded for lunch. May, Izzie and I chucked all our stuff into our bags and raced off to find Sienna. Our first stop was the medical room, and there we found Sienna lying on one of the beds, reading a magazine, a can of Coke beside her.

'Oh, hi, girls.' Sienna stretched lazily, like a cat. 'Enjoy the rest of your maths class?'

'Were you *really* ill?' Izzie blurted out.

Sienna looked extremely amused. 'What do *you* think?' She finished her Coke and lobbed the can neatly into the wastepaper basket. 'Come on, let's eat. I'm starving.'

And she strolled out of the room. Izzie, May and I followed her obediently – like little lambs, I guess. But Sienna was *so* different from all the other girls at Bramfield that the three of us were totally bewitched by her. Even though she'd only known us for a couple of weeks, it was obvious that Sienna was becoming the leader of our little gang.

'I've got to go to the library and do some research

for my history essay after lunch,' Izzie remarked gloomily as we went to the school dining hall. 'Otherwise I won't be able to hand it in on time, and you know how scary Mrs Cairns is if you don't do your homework. God, I hate the Tudors!'

'Oh, no, *don't*,' Sienna cried. 'That's *so* boring!' She linked arms with Izzie and Izzie flushed, looking pleased. 'I want you to help me with netball practice. I'm thinking of trying out for the school team.'

'Well, OK,' Izzie agreed.

'Fab.' Sienna smiled and walked off towards the dining hall with Izzie, leaving me and May behind.

'Why is Sienna so keen on Izzie all of a sudden?' May commented, sounding a bit jealous. 'Izzie's not even any good at netball!'

'Come on,' I said, avoiding the question. 'We'd better go into lunch.'

As we followed Sienna and Izzie into the dining hall, I became aware of a vague, uneasy feeling lying like a heavy stone in the bottom of my tummy. I had begun to realise that Sienna seemed to have the gift of being able to make everyone do *exactly* what she wanted. It was also impossible to know when she was lying and when she was telling the truth.

Suddenly I thought of my football mates. Grace,

Hannah, Katy, Lauren and Georgie all had their faults, sure they did – and so did I! – but I knew I could trust them. And even though Katy didn't want to talk about her home life, she was still open and honest and direct about everything else. None of them mystified and unsettled me, and left me feeling slightly nervous like Sienna did.

Now you're just being melodramatic, Jasmin Sharma, I scoffed silently. *Stop being so OTT*. But however much I told myself not to be so daft, I couldn't shake off the nagging feeling that maybe being friends with Sienna wasn't going to be as wonderful as I'd thought...

'More fractions!' I groaned, handing my maths homework to Hannah, who was sprawled out on my bed. It was later that day, and the six of us were having our usual Friday evening get-together before the match on Saturday. We usually met up at the local park, but the rain was tipping down, so I'd invited them to mine instead.

'It's fine,' Hannah said, patting my arm. 'I like fractions. They're kind of like working out puzzles.'

'I'm worried about you, Hannah.' Lauren laid her hand on Hannah's forehead and frowned. 'Yep, you're definitely feverish and you need to see your doctor ASAP.'

'I think she's quite mad, frankly,' Georgie added, as, counting under her breath, Hannah scribbled down one of the answers. 'But if it keeps Jasmin in the Stars, hey, who cares?'

'Shouldn't Jasmin be doing some of that, though, Hannah?' Grace asked. 'I don't think you should be writing down *all* the answers for her.'

'Of course not,' I gabbled, embarrassed. 'I *will* do some of it myself. It's just that—'

'Jas, I'm not having a go,' Grace broke in. 'It's just that you'll *never* get any better at maths if Hannah does all the work for you.'

'You know,' Lauren began, 'it might just be easier if you had this out with your parents once and for all, Jasmin—'

'No way!' I snapped. 'And any way, what are *you* giving me advice for? You didn't tell your parents for ages that *you* were unhappy because they were working all the time!'

Lauren looked a bit upset, and I couldn't believe I'd had a dig at her like that. It just wasn't like me at all.

'Sorry, Lauren.' Tears in my eyes, I flew across my

bedroom and gave her a big hug. To my relief, she hugged me warmly back.

'It's OK, Jas,' Lauren said. 'But I *did* tell them in the end, and that's when things started to get better.'

'It's so *hard*, though,' I sighed. 'They're all excited about the new firm being a success so they're at the office a lot, and I don't see them so much at the moment. I need to find the right time. And besides, I just don't know what to say.'

'*I hate maths* would be a great start,' Georgie remarked.

'What about the maths tutor your parents were talking about?' Katy was standing by Ludmilla's cage, feeding her a raisin. 'Is that still going to happen?'

'I don't know,' I sighed. 'If it does, at least Mrs Rehman will help me to catch up. I know I can't rely on Hannah forever. But I *can't* give up on the Stars.'

'I should think not!' Georgie exclaimed indignantly, chucking a pillow at me. 'If you do, I'll *never* speak to you again, Jasmin Sharma!'

'Every cloud has a silver lining,' Hannah remarked, which sent us all into fits of laughter, even Georgie.

Suddenly my bedroom door opened. I almost *wet* myself. Instantly Hannah threw my maths homework and the pen she was holding under my bed. At least, she tried to, but missed. Georgie was sitting on the floor below her and almost got stabbed in the eye by the pen. My maths homework cascaded down onto the floor, and Lauren slid off the bed and sat on top of it to hide it from view.

A second later, Mum stuck her head in.

'Hi, girls,' she said cheerfully. 'How are you?'

'Fine,' the others chorused. Meanwhile, I tried to calm myself down. I was sure that my face was bright red with guilt.

'Jasmin, I've just been speaking to Mrs Horowitz,' Mum began.

'Did you just say *Mrs Horror Witch*, Mrs Sharma?' Georgie enquired innocently. Naughty girl! She knows very well that's Mrs Horowitz's nickname. But at least it made me smile, which probably made me look a little less guilty.

'No, Mrs Horowitz,' Mum said. 'H-o-r-o-w-i-t-z. She's the head of maths at Bramfield.' She beamed at me. 'I'm sure you won't mind me saying this in front of your friends, Jasmin, because Mrs Horowitz has just been telling me that your maths is slowly improving. So, well done, darling.'

'Thanks, Mum,' I muttered, knowing that it was only because of Hannah's help that I was hanging on in there by my fingernails. I still wasn't out of the danger zone yet, though – because as far as I knew, the extra tuition during the Christmas holidays was still on. And if Mum and Dad decided that I had to carry on *after* Christmas too, then I really *would* have to fight to be allowed to stay with the Stars.

Oh, maybe Lauren and the others were right. Perhaps it *was* time to have a serious talk with my parents. But the thought made me feel sick with nerves. I knew they'd be *so* disappointed in me, and that was the worst thing to bear.

'By the way, Jasmin, I almost forgot.' Mum had been halfway out of the door when she stopped again. 'I popped in to tell you that your gran's coming to stay with us tomorrow for a few weeks.'

My heart sank like a very large stone.

'Oh, great,' I said breezily.

'Spill it,' Georgie ordered as Mum shut the door behind her. 'What's with your gran, Jasmin?'

'Yep, you should have seen your face,' Lauren

remarked. 'You looked like your mum had invited Dracula to stay.'

I heaved a sigh. 'I don't think any of you have met my gran, have you?'

'No, is she very scary?' Katy asked.

'Not really.' I forced a rueful grin. 'She *can* be really sweet and funny and a great laugh, and I *do* love her to bits. But guess what? Hello, another accountant and maths genius in the house! That's all I need…'

The others looked dismayed.

'Gran's never shy about saying what she thinks, either,' I went on gloomily. 'She's always telling Mum and Dad her opinions. And she's *never* liked me playing football, for one thing.'

'Neither does *my* gran,' Lauren put in, with a mischievous twinkle in her eye. 'So mostly I ignore her.'

'Well, it's difficult to ignore *my* gran,' I sighed. 'And I just *know* what's going to happen. When she finds out I've got to have extra maths tuition at Christmas, she'll say that I spend too much time on other stuff. Like football, for instance.'

'No problem,' Georgie said confidently. 'All we have to do is make sure that Hannah keeps on helping you. Then, if you're doing OK in maths, your gran *can't* say you have to give up the Stars.'

I was silent. I could see now that I really *didn't* have a choice. There was no way I could confess all to Mum and Dad, not with Gran sticking her nose in as I knew she would. She'd probably tell them that the reason I wasn't that great at maths was because my head was full of other, useless things like *football*.

'Don't look so down, Jasmin.' Hannah slipped her arm around my shoulders. 'We'll all help you any way we can.'

I nodded and managed a faint grin. I had no idea what was going to happen, but I just wanted to be certain that I'd still be a Springhill Stars player after Christmas.

Right now, though, I just wasn't sure.

CHAPTER FOUR

'Everybody back to help out!' Georgie shouted, looking a bit panicked. I raced towards our goal with Lauren, Hannah, Emily and Ruby. Meanwhile, one of the Bees midfielders – the one who'd been running rings around us Stars players like we didn't exist – scooted over to take their corner.

God, the away match this morning was a tough one. It was a windy autumn day with horrible, drizzly rain, but the action had been so full-on since the start of the game, I'd hardly noticed. The Burnlee Bees were fifth in our league, only six points behind us, and they were determined to beat us and grab those precious points. We were just as determined to beat *them*, though, in order to keep up with the Belles. We'd had chances too – Grace had hit the post and Lauren had headed just over. But the Bees had also had their moments. Amelia, the annoying midfielder who was just *too* good, had almost scored twice. Both times Georgie's brilliant saves had kept the game at 0-0, though.

We all squeezed into the box, waiting for the corner. There was a complete sea of purple Stars shirts, and yellow and black Bees jostling for position. Colour clash nightmare!

'Keep your eyes on the ball,' Georgie muttered to me, Katy and Jo-Jo, who were grouped around her.

Amelia took the corner and whipped the ball into our box. At first I thought it was heading for one of the Bees' strikers, so I dashed towards the girl nearest me to stop her getting it. But suddenly a gust of wind made the ball swerve wildly. It changed direction slightly and sailed over everyone's heads towards the goal. Out of the corner of my eye, I saw Georgie leap for it, miss and tumble over. Then the ball dipped down just below the crossbar and fell into the net.

'*Noooooo!*' I groaned as the Bees began celebrating madly.

'Foul!' Georgie gasped, jumping to her feet.

And it was! I just hadn't heard the referee's whistle. One of the Bees strikers had climbed all over Georgie while trying to get to the ball, and had knocked her over. Whoo-hoo! Goal disallowed!

'That was lucky,' I gasped with relief.

'Yeah, I'd rather be fouled and lose my front teeth than lose a goal,' Georgie declared as she ran to get the ball to take the free kick. I don't think she was joking, either!

The game continued. It was real end-to-end stuff. One minute the Stars had the ball and were racing towards the Bees' goal, then a few seconds later the Bees won the ball back and headed in the opposite direction. It must have been quite exciting for the people watching, but for us it was hell. Every time the Bees got the ball, my heart jumped into my mouth. Ria had told us at half-time that the Belles were already four goals up against the bottom team in the league, the Fairmount Foxes, so we knew *they* weren't going to lose today. That meant we had to win too, or fall further behind them in the league table. If the score stayed at 0-0, we'd only get one point, and that meant the Belles would grab another three for beating the Foxes and widen the gap between us.

The Bees goalie took a run-up and whacked the ball as hard as she could. She didn't get much of a lift on it, though, and it dropped down right at Lauren's feet. Lauren immediately dashed back towards the Bees' goal, dribbling the ball neatly in front of her.

As Hannah, Emily, Ruby and I scurried after her, I glanced ahead to see where Grace was. But as usual, she was flanked by two Bees defenders. They'd pretty much marked her out of the game today, knowing what a great striker she was. Lauren hesitated, holding the ball up while she waited for us to come alongside, but a Bees player was bearing down on her so she was forced to pass back to me. I groaned under my breath as I realised that the Bees were trapping us in midfield with nowhere to go. Curses!

Suddenly, though, there was a blur of purple as Katy streaked past us all on the wing, pushing up from defence. I booted the ball towards her, and it was a *perfect* pass, though I say so myself! Straight into her path so that she didn't even have to break stride to collect the ball.

'Go on!' I could hear Georgie yelling as Katy dummied a flustered Bees defender and continued racing towards their end. 'Get in there, you lot!'

Katy was almost at the corner flag now as Hannah, Lauren, Ruby and I joined Grace in the box. For a moment we thought she'd lost the ball as a Bees defender blocked her, but somehow Katy managed to get the cross in. It was hard and low, but Ruby stuck her foot out, and—

'Goal!' I roared with delight as the ball smashed into the net.

It was the Stars who were celebrating now, and it was for real this time. *One-nil, one-nil, one-nil, one-nil!*

Poor old Ruby had almost collapsed under the weight of hugs and back slaps as we all crowded around her.

'Concentrate!' Georgie yelled from the other end of the pitch. She'd celebrated by throwing her baseball cap into the air and I noticed it had got stuck on top of the net! 'There's still ten minutes to go.'

The Bees were looking a bit down-in-the-mouth as they kicked off again, and I hoped that meant they'd given up on equalising. No way, though! A scorching shot from their midfielder, Amelia, in the last few minutes was luckily blocked by Katy, and booted away downfield.

'God, I'm glad that's over!' Grace panted as the ref blew the final whistle. 'That was a close one.'

'Thanks to Katy,' Georgie said, patting her on the back.

Katy had rolled one of her socks down and was examining a big red patch on her leg, where'd she'd stopped the ball. 'I'll have a gorgeous black and blue bruise there tomorrow,' she said, wincing. 'But it was worth it!'

Ria came over to say well done, and then, aching, wet and muddy, we headed off the pitch in one big crowd to dry off and get changed. As we did so, I remembered that my dad would have arrived with Gran by the time I got home, and my mood dimmed a little. Gran could be really lovely – when she wasn't being bossy and we *weren't* talking about maths. But I had a yucky feeling that maths was *all* anyone was going to be talking about for the next few weeks.

'What are we doing tomorrow?' Lauren asked as we stripped off our kits in the changing-room. 'Do you want to come round to mine? If the weather's rubbish, we can stay in and play on the Wii or watch DVDs.'

'Cool, I'm in.' Grace began brushing out her silky

blonde hair. 'I'm going to see my dad in the morning, but I'll be OK for the afternoon.'

'Me too,' Hannah agreed.

'I'm not sure,' Katy said with a frown. 'I *should* be able to come, but I'll text you if I can't, Lauren.'

'I'm up for anything that gets me out of the house tomorrow.' Georgie pulled a face. 'I think Ria's coming round to have Sunday lunch with Dad.'

'Jasmin?' Lauren was staring at me enquiringly.

'Um – I'll try to come,' I said, 'if I can get away from my gran!'

'Bring her over to mine,' Lauren suggested, her blue eyes twinkling mischievously. 'She can have a go on the Wii.'

'Don't,' I groaned. 'I've seen Gran in action on Dan's Xbox before. She's a demon.' I slung on my bright pink jacket, and knotted my silver glittery wool scarf around my neck. 'See you, guys. I'd better run. Mum told me *not* to be late.'

Everyone yelled goodbye as I scooted out of the changing-room. I was so glad we'd won the game against the Bees. If we'd lost, it would have been a real downer for the rest of the weekend. And as it was, the weekend was looking like the mega-pits, any way. Gran was going to be on my case about maths as soon as she arrived. And I had that history essay to do about the Tudors, the one that Izzie had been getting into such a flap about. I hadn't even started it yet, and it had to be handed in on Monday. Still, at least Hannah had finished off my maths homework for me on Friday night. As I headed across the car park towards my mum's new car, I pushed away the familiar feeling of guilt that made me feel sick to my stomach…

'Your dad's arrived home with Gran,' Mum said, flipping her mobile shut. 'I just got a call.'

'Great,' I said, buckling my seat belt.

'Jasmin, you know your gran's got a few health problems?' Mum went on. 'Her cholesterol and blood pressure are a bit high, and her doctor's said she ought to try and lose some weight. We're going to be living on healthy meals like salad for the next few weeks while she's here, so no complaints, OK?'

'OK,' I agreed quietly. *Definitely* not a good time to be announcing I hated maths, then. I didn't want to send Gran's blood pressure shooting through the roof!

I expected Mum to start up the car, but she didn't. Instead she turned to look at me.

'Jasmin, are you all right?' she asked, frowning

ever so slightly. 'You don't seem quite yourself these days.'

Should I say something? Right now?

I didn't know what to do. Maybe I *would* have blurted out the whole sorry story then, if Gran hadn't already arrived. I just *knew*, though, that Mum and Dad would discuss it with her, and that Gran would be all for me giving up football to make time for extra maths tuition. And I was absolutely sure that none of them would believe that I didn't like maths, was no good at it and didn't want to be an accountant when I left school. They'd just think I was being dippy, ditsy, day-dreamy Jasmin who just didn't want to work hard in class.

'Don't worry, I'm fine, Mum,' I told her. 'I've just got a lot on at the moment.'

Ooh, Jasmin Sharma, you opened your mouth without putting your brain in gear!

'Well, that's what your dad and I are worried about,' Mum shot back immediately as we pulled out of the car park. 'What with all your outside interests, we think your work has been suffering.'

By *work*, Mum meant *maths*, of course. For God's sake, I was getting As in English, drama and art, and quite good marks in history and my other subjects too. OK, to be honest, *not* in geography, because I can hardly find my way to the end of our street, never mind remember where the Limpopo River is! But I really *wasn't* doing too badly. It was just my parents who seemed to have tunnel vision where maths was concerned.

'Look, Mum, it's *fine*,' I repeated, desperately trying to fight my corner. 'I know art club's after school on Mondays, but it's only for an hour. And I joined the drama group too late this term to get a part in the Christmas panto, so I'm only painting scenery, and I'm doing that in my lunch breaks. And you know football helps to keep me fit...'

'Hm.' Mum was still frowning. 'Your dad and I just think you're too busy, sweetie, and that at some point, things will have to change.'

'You said I had to improve my maths, and I *have*,' I interrupted her.

'Yes, but will it last?' Mum wanted to know. 'We can arrange extra tuition over the Christmas holidays, but what about after that? If you have to continue with Mrs Rehman, then you definitely can't carry on with all these other activities.'

I was silent as we drew up outside the house. That was the problem. How long could I go on relying on

Hannah to help me out? I was getting into really deep water, and with a feeling of dread, I knew it.

When we went into the house, Dad, Kallie, Shanti, Dan and Gran were in the living room. They were all chattering away loudly at the same time, hardly listening to what any of the others were saying. That's my family for you!

'Jasmin, my darling, I'm hearing great things about your maths,' was the first thing Gran said to me as she jumped up and gave me a huge, bone-crushing hug. She's tall and well-built like Dad, with long black hair streaked with grey piled up on top of her head. Sometimes she wears saris and shalwaar kameez, but today she had on black trousers and a funky, chunky raspberry-coloured belted cardigan. 'Tell me more.'

'Well, we've been studying fractions for the last few weeks,' I explained, trying to sound enthusiastic as I chucked my sports bag behind the sofa. 'I think I'm doing OK.' *Thanks to Hannah…*

'Ah, fractions!' Gran looked quite excited. *WHY? Can someone please tell me why fractions are so thrilling to so many people?* 'But they're so easy. When are you going to get onto some really tough stuff?'

'Yeah, like algebra,' Dan, who was sprawled on the sofa, added.

'Algebra – tough?' Gran replied briskly, slapping Dan on the shoulder. 'Nonsense! Wait till you start advanced calculus.'

'Have you done Pythagoras yet?' Kallie asked me. 'I thought that was really cool.'

'What is it, some kind of yoga?' I said, trying to make a joke of it. Who or what the hell was Pythagoras? I had *no* idea.

'Oh, Jas, you're so funny!' Kallie giggled.

Gran threw her arm around my shoulders and gave me another squeeze. 'While I'm here, I'll give you some maths tuition, Jasmin. We'll start tomorrow afternoon with some easy algebra, and by the time you do it in class, you'll be well ahead of everyone else.'

'Fab,' I said weakly. There went my girlie Sunday afternoon with the others, right out of the window. Some tuition from Gran *might* be a good thing, I supposed, but whenever any of the family had tried to help me in the past, it had always ended in tears. Mine! All because they didn't seem able to come down to my level, which was very low (meaning, complete dumbo).

'Now, Ma, you're supposed to be resting,' Dad warned. Gran shot him a withering look.

'My cholesterol level is a little high, and so is my blood pressure,' Gran snorted. 'It doesn't mean I'm on my deathbed, you know. I hardly think spending two or three enjoyable hours studying maths with one of my darling grandchildren is going to make me keel over.'

Two or three hours? I just about managed to stop *myself* from keeling over!

'Did you win today, Jammy?' Dan asked.

I nodded. 'One-nil.'

Gran tutted loudly. 'Still playing football? I'm sure there are *lots* more useful things you could be doing, Jasmin—'

'Mum, I'm starving,' I broke in. I didn't want to give Gran a chance to get started. 'When's lunch? I want to start my history essay this afternoon.'

'In about fifteen minutes,' Mum replied.

'What are we having?' Gran asked eagerly. 'Curry and rice?'

Mum shook her head. 'Chicken salad.'

'Rabbit food!' Gran grumbled, flouncing over to the TV.

I slipped quietly out of the room. As I'd known all

along, Gran would *definitely* be shouting very loudly that I ought to be thinking about giving up football. It was yet another complication I could do without.

Glumly I took my phone out of my pocket and texted Lauren.

Soz, can't make 2moz. Gran giving me maths tuition – heeeeelp!

'Right, try the next one.' Gran wrote down a sum on the paper in front of her, then pushed it across to me.

$6a - 4 (x 2a) = ?$

I stared at it in frustration, getting hot and sweaty all over and wishing I was a million miles away (or at least at Lauren's house with the other girls). We'd been doing this stuff for the last hour since Sunday lunch finished. At first it had been pretty easy: things like $a - 7 = 14$. Even *I* could do that, although I didn't let Gran see that I was secretly counting on my fingers underneath the table! But as soon as she started making the sums harder, I could feel my brain begin to overheat and refuse to co-operate.

'Um, let me see...' I said, in what I hoped was an intelligent manner. Gran had explained several times, at super-speed, how to work these sums out only a few minutes ago. But the problem was that I just *couldn't* remember. It was always the same with maths, even if I understood it a little first time round – all explanations seemed to go in one of my ears and straight out of the other.

Jasmin + maths = disaster.

That was one sum I had no problem working out!

I sat there staring at the piece of paper. I knew I had to work out what number *a* represented, but the possibilities just seemed too enormous.

Oh, the doorbell! Saved!

'I'll go,' I gabbled, leaping up from my chair and almost tripping over in my haste to get away. Everyone else had gone out, so there was only me and Gran at home.

I raced to the front door and flung it open. I was amazed to find Lauren, Grace, Georgie, Katy and Hannah outside.

'Surprise!' they chorused, beaming at me.

'Oh, guys, am I glad to see you,' I wailed, flinging my arms out to hug them all. 'I'm dying here. Algebra is killing me!'

'Poor Jas.' Grace patted me on the back.

'We're on our way to the park for a kick-around

now the weather's a bit better,' Lauren added. She was throwing a football from hand to hand. 'Want to come?'

'Ooh, do I!' I groaned longingly. 'But I'm not sure Gran will let me. Especially if she knows we're going to play footie.'

I heard footsteps behind me and turned to find Gran heading down the hall towards us. Lauren panicked and immediately shoved the ball out of sight into a large shrub next to the door. It was *so* funny I almost giggled, but managed not to.

'Hello,' Gran said, raising her eyebrows. 'What are your friends doing here, Jasmin?'

'We were just wondering if Jasmin would like to come for a walk with us,' Georgie replied, a supremely innocent look on her face. 'We're going on a nature ramble through the park. To look at plants and trees and birds and stuff.'

Gran hesitated. 'Well, we *were* in the middle of a maths session...'

'I could do with a bit of fresh air, Gran,' I said eagerly. *Pleeeeeze, let me go! Before I faint with boredom!*

'All right, Jasmin,' Gran agreed. 'We'll carry on when you get back. But don't be too long, OK?'

'No, Gran,' I promised. Grinning madly at the girls, I grabbed my jacket and ran out of the house before Gran could change her mind. Lauren retrieved the ball and we all scuttled off down the path.

'Thanks, guys,' I said gratefully. I was really touched by their loyalty, and the fact that they'd come to save me. 'I think my brain would have gone up in flames if you lot hadn't arrived.'

'What were you and your gran doing?' Hannah asked.

'Algebra!' I moaned. 'Horrible, horrible algebra. The sums don't even have proper numbers in them – you have to work out what a and x and y stand for. Nightmare!'

'So you're no closer to telling your parents how you feel about maths, then,' Katy remarked.

'No, I can't do it while Gran's here,' I explained. 'My mum and dad listen to everything she says, so that'll be the end for me and the Stars if Gran gets involved.' We turned into the park gates, making our way towards our favourite footie pitch. 'Anyway, she's only here for a few weeks. Then I'll see.'

'I can't stay long,' Grace said as Lauren chucked

the ball onto the pitch. 'I've got homework to finish for tomorrow.'

'Homework is the invention of the devil.' Georgie ran after the ball and side-footed it to me. 'I think we should start a campaign to get it banned.'

'Well, I might be rubbish at maths, but at least I've done my history essay,' I said proudly, sliding the ball to Katy. 'It took me *ages*.'

'I like history.' Katy shielded the ball neatly from Georgie who was trying to rob her, and flicked it to Hannah. 'English history is so crazy – all those people chopping off each other's heads.'

'I actually quite like history too,' I confessed. 'Except we have this *really* grumpy teacher called Mrs Cairns. She has a massive fit if you don't give your homework in on time. I don't think even Sienna would like to get on the wrong side of *her*.'

'Sienna? Is that your new mate at school?' Lauren asked as Katy passed to her.

I nodded and told them the story of how Sienna's dog had apparently eaten her homework. The others thought this was hilarious.

'*So* cool,' Grace remarked. 'I didn't think anyone would ever *dare* use that excuse.'

'She must have some nerve,' Georgie said admiringly.

'Oh, Sienna's all that, and more,' I replied with a grin. 'You'll have to meet her sometime.'

I meant it, too. In all the kerfuffle about Gran arriving, I'd forgotten the slightly uneasy feelings I'd had about Sienna. I'd decided that I *had* been a bit OTT really, and I *was* looking forward to seeing what the other girls would make of her.

But that was before what happened on Monday morning.

It was *horrible*...

'Did you have a good weekend, girls?' Sienna asked me, Izzie and May as we strolled down the corridor towards our next lesson. It was history, and I'd have preferred *not* to be strolling at all, more like hurrying as fast as my legs could carry me without actually running, which wasn't allowed. Mrs Cairns was always *totally* ticked off if any of us arrived after she did, but Sienna wasn't hurrying for *anybody*.

'Yep, we won our match one-nil,' I replied.

'No, I spent ages on that stupid history essay,' Izzie moaned.

'Have you done *yours*, Sienna?' May asked.

'Of course.' Sienna shrugged her shoulders. 'My

dog doesn't eat every bit of my homework, you know. Only the stuff I haven't bothered to do.'

Izzie, May and I giggled. As we reached the classroom door, I spotted Mrs Cairns coming from the opposite direction. We slipped into the room a few seconds before her, and I breathed a sigh of relief. Being mates with Sienna was fun, but it could also be slightly scary.

'Sit down, girls.' Mrs Cairns put her briefcase down on her desk with a thump. 'Latisha, collect up the homework essays, please.'

I opened my bag to get my essay out. I'd put it on top of everything else in a plastic folder, to protect it.

But it wasn't there.

You know how your mind starts to swim and your tummy sinks and you think you're seeing things because you just *know* something can't be right? Well, that was exactly how I felt. My essay had been there this morning when I packed my bag for school. But now it wasn't.

Maybe it had slipped lower down into the bag...

I began pulling out books and pencil-cases and paper and tissues and all the other stuff I cart around with me, piling it up on the table.

'What's the matter, Jasmin?' Izzie whispered as Latisha Collins went around the classroom, collecting up the essays.

'I can't find my homework!' I whispered back.

I went through all my files and folders and textbooks but still I couldn't find it. By now I was so hot and flustered, I practically had steam coming out of my ears. And Latisha was getting closer.

Desperately I tipped out the rest of the contents of my bag onto the table. In my agitation, I knocked one of my folders onto the floor and the papers spilled out everywhere, just as Latisha stopped in front of me.

'Jasmin, what *are* you doing?' Mrs Cairns enquired.

'Looking for my homework, Miss,' I replied breathlessly, crawling around under the table to pick everything up. 'I *know* I put it in my bag this morning.'

There was a tense silence in the classroom as I continued to sort through all my bits and pieces. That stupid essay had to be here *somewhere*, I thought, biting my lip. Latisha, Izzie and May were staring at me sympathetically as, near to tears, I started going through everything for the second time.

'Maybe you didn't bring it to school, Jasmin,' Mrs Cairns observed frostily.

'I *did*, Miss,' I protested.

'Well, you don't appear to have it now.' Mrs Cairns shot me a glare. 'You know my rules. That means detention for you today at lunchtime—'

'Just a moment, Miss.' Sienna bent down and picked something up from under the table. 'Is *this* it, Jasmin?'

She was holding my essay in its protective plastic pocket, and I almost *cried* with relief.

'Yes, that's it!' I gasped.

Sienna winked at me and handed the essay to Latisha along with her own.

'Put your things away quickly, then, Jasmin,' Mrs Cairns told me. 'We've wasted enough time already.'

I began stuffing everything back into my bag. But as I did so, something struck me. Where, exactly, had Sienna "found" my essay? I'd crawled under the table to pick up the sheets that had fallen out of my folder, but I knew I hadn't left anything behind.

A horrible suspicion popped into my head. Very slightly I leaned over so that I could see Sienna's bag. It was open, almost as if she'd just unzipped it and taken my essay out.

Had Sienna stolen my essay from my bag earlier and kept it until now?

I told you it was horrible. I *hated* thinking things like that about someone who was supposed to be a mate, but what other explanation could there be? Maybe Sienna had done it for a laugh, but how could she find it funny when I'd been so panicked about the whole situation?

I couldn't concentrate at all in class, and that meant a couple more sarky comments from Mrs Cairns, but all I could think about was Sienna. When the bell finally rang for our next lesson, I just couldn't hold back.

'Did *you* hide my essay, Sienna?' I blurted out as the four of us went down the corridor.

Izzie and May looked shocked, but Sienna smiled.

'It was just a joke, Jasmin,' she said calmly. 'You should have seen your face – it was *so* funny!'

'But you got me into trouble!' I spluttered, outraged.

'No, I didn't,' Sienna pointed out. 'You didn't get a detention, did you?'

'No, but—'

'Well, chill out, then.' Sienna yawned, very deliberately. 'It was a joke, that's all. That's what mates do, play jokes on each other. No harm done.'

This just didn't feel right to me. I couldn't see *any* of my other mates playing *this* kind of joke. I glanced at Izzie and May for support, but was a bit surprised to see that neither of them could meet my gaze.

'Like Sienna says, you didn't get into any trouble, Jasmin,' May muttered. 'Don't get so wound up about it.'

I didn't know what to say. I just felt that Sienna's idea of a joke was mean and a bit spiteful, especially as we all knew how scary Mrs Cairns could be.

'Come on, Jasmin.' Sienna linked her arm through mine. 'I'll buy you a choccie bar at lunch to make it up to you.' She laughed. 'But it really *was* funny. Your face – I thought you were going to faint with panic!'

This time Izzie and May laughed too. I didn't. I longed to pull my arm away from Sienna's, but I didn't have the courage. Was I reacting too much to what Sienna had insisted was a harmless joke among friends? I wasn't sure. But I *did* know that this wasn't the kind of prank I'd have played on any of *my* mates, like Georgie or Katy or any of the other girls, and they wouldn't have done it to me, either. It was just a bit too nasty.

But then, that was Sienna. Beautiful, interesting

and charming, she could also be nerve-wracking, unpredictable and scary. And I was realising that, even though she'd been my friend since the day she'd arrived at Bramfield, I didn't really know her at all.

CHAPTER FIVE

'Good stuff, Jasmin,' Ria called approvingly as I hit a shot past Georgie and the ball crashed into the net. 'Nice to see you're on form tonight!'

I grinned. Our Tuesday night training session was nearly over, and we were finishing off with some shooting practice before we went to get changed. I was feeling happier tonight, although nothing much had changed. It was just so *fab* to be with Lauren, Hannah, Grace, Katy and Georgie. Kicking a ball around and enjoying my footie and having a laugh and just being ME. I don't know what I'd have done without the Stars. Hannah helping me with my maths had taken some of the pressure off me too. But Gran was still banging on about giving me more maths tuition, as well as moaning about me coming to training tonight. I'd been *so* worried that she might tell Mum and Dad I ought to stay home, that I'd hardly dared to *breathe* until Georgie and her dad had come to pick me up and I was safely out of the house.

And then, at school, there was Sienna. She'd been really full-on nice to me since our history lesson the previous day. She'd bought me a bar of chocolate and she wanted me to sit next to her in all our classes we had and she was being – oh, *so* bright and funny and sweet and kind to me. It was obvious that Izzie and May were a bit jealous. I couldn't help liking Sienna all over again, and forgiving her for the "joke". And yet something still didn't feel quite right...

'Got any maths homework tonight, Jasmin?' Hannah asked me as we piled into the changing-room.

'Yep, 'fraid so,' I said. 'I brought it with me.'

I dived into my bag, pulled out my homework and handed it to Hannah.

'Shall I call you later, so we can go through it together?' I went on.

'Sorry, Jasmin, I can't.' Hannah had produced

a pen and was already scribbling away, deep in calculations. 'I'm going over to see my grandpa now. But I'll just do some of them for you, and then you can copy the way I've worked them out.'

'OK,' I agreed.

I was wondering whether to go ahead and tell the other girls about Sienna and ask them what they thought about her "joke". But now that I'd calmed down, it seemed a bit mean to moan about my school friends to my football mates. So I decided not to. After all, now that Sienna had seen how much she'd upset me, I didn't think she'd ever do anything like that again.

Or would she?

Because we were messing around and having a laugh, it took us ages to get changed. Lauren had got some slinky new red shoes with a high heel that her mum had brought home from the fashion store where she works, and we all wanted to try them on. Even Georgie had a go, and we almost *died* laughing watching her try to walk in them. She only managed to totter about three steps before she collapsed and fell against me.

'Oh, you're a hopeless case, Georgie!' I exclaimed. 'Let *me* have a go.'

Georgie passed the shoes over and I sat down and slipped them on. They were gorgeous, but the heels were *really* high. I stood up gingerly – and almost fell over before I'd taken a single step! Of course, Georgie, Lauren, Grace and Katy burst into uncontrollable giggles.

It was only about twenty minutes later, when I was almost ready to go, that I remembered Hannah and my maths homework. I glanced over, and there was Hannah sitting there in her Stars shirt and pink knickers (she'd taken her shorts off, and that was all!), scribbling away.

'Hannah!' I squeaked apologetically. 'You're not still doing my maths, are you?'

'Sorry, I got a bit carried away.' Hannah handed me the homework, then dragged her shirt over her head. 'I've left a few for you to work out yourself, though.'

I glanced at the sums. Almost all of them had been done, with the calculations included down the side. I felt a rush of relief, mixed with enormous guilt.

'Hannah, you're a star,' I said gratefully. Without Hannah's help, it would have taken me all evening to struggle through the sums, and I still had other homework to finish too. But I felt bad about it, nevertheless.

Hannah shrugged. 'No probs.'

'Don't forget, Hannah can't help you out forever, Jasmin,' Grace reminded me.

'Tell me about it,' I muttered. 'I know I can't expect Han to do my maths homework all the way up to my GCSEs!'

'Look, it's only for a little while,' Lauren broke in. 'Just to get you through a difficult time while your gran's here. We're all right behind you, Jas.'

'I know.' I brightened up a little. 'I love you guys, thanks *so* much.'

'I have to leave *now* before we all start crying and hugging each other,' Georgie said with a grin. 'Ready, Jasmin?'

I nodded. I said goodbye to the others, with a special hug for Hannah, even though Georgie pulled a face! Then Georgie and I headed for the car park.

'Try not to stress too much, Jasmin,' Georgie advised me. 'You're just doing what you have to, for the moment. Something'll change, and then things will sort themselves out.'

'Oh, yeah?' I grinned at her. 'Where's the *old*

Georgie, the one who couldn't wait for anything and wanted things, like, right now?'

'Maybe I'm growing up,' Georgie suggested solemnly. She stopped in front of the college notice board and glanced over her shoulder to make sure that no one was around. Then she whipped a pen out of her tracksuit pocket and drew a pair of huge glasses, a moustache and beard on a photocopied picture of the college principal (who was a woman!). 'Nope, maybe not!'

I could hardly walk, I was laughing so hard. Georgie looked quite pleased with herself for cheering me up even more.

'I reckon we'll beat the Grantfield Gazelles on Saturday, no problem,' Georgie said as we went to find her dad in the car park. 'And the Belles *might* just draw with the Swallows.'

So then Georgie and I got involved in a discussion about Saturday's game while Mr Taylor drove us home. We got really into it, so I was feeling all bouncy and upbeat when we arrived at my place.

'Jasmin, did you finish your maths homework?' Mum asked as soon as I got in through the front door. She and Gran were watching a Bollywood movie on TV.

'Nearly,' I called back. Well, it was true. Hannah *had* left some of the sums for me to do myself, hadn't she? 'Oh, great – I love this film! It has *the* best music!'

Just then the film's hero and heroine launched into my favourite song and dance routine so I joined in enthusiastically, miming the words and copying the moves. Mum and Gran thought this was hysterical!

'By the way, Jasmin, your mum and I would like to see your homework when you've finished it,' Gran chimed in halfway through the song.

That stopped me dancing straight away!

'Sure,' I said casually, really thinking, *Oh, bum!* I made myself a quick cheese sandwich and then scooted upstairs. Quickly I up-ended my bag, found Hannah's piece of paper and copied down all the answers she'd worked out for me while I ate my sarnie. There were three sums she hadn't done, so I tried to work them out quickly, using Hannah's method plus my calculator. Of course I got hopelessly confused, and I ended up panicking and simply guessing the answer to the last one. Then I took a deep breath and strolled downstairs carrying my homework, trying to look all cool and calm.

I'd hoped Mum and Gran had forgotten about

me, but they were waiting in the living room with mugs of hot chocolate. I handed my homework over.

'Good,' Mum said, sounding a little surprised. 'Not bad at all, Jasmin. Only a couple wrong. These last two, right at the end.'

'Really?' I perked up instantly. That meant of the three sums I'd done myself, I'd actually got one of them right. Yay, me!

'Of course, there's no reason why you should get *any* of them wrong,' Gran added, studying my calculations closely. 'That's the beauty of maths. Once you know the formula for working things out, it's easy-peasy.'

Yeah, right, I thought. But I didn't say that. I don't have a death wish!

'Any biscuits to have with this hot chocolate?' Gran asked.

'No, sorry,' Mum replied firmly. 'I must say, Jasmin, I'm a bit taken aback by how much you've improved over the last three weeks,' she went on, handing my homework back to me. I was alarmed. Was there a touch of suspicion in her manner, or was I imagining it?

'Yes, what's changed, Jasmin?' Gran was giving me that laser-eyed look of hers, the one that makes you think she can see right through you. I didn't want to tell fibs and I was feeling a strong urge to confess all because I'm a *hopeless* liar. But if I did, I would lose everything I loved doing, like playing for the Stars. I might also get Hannah into trouble too, if my parents complained to hers.

'I'm getting a lot more help,' I said carefully. 'Miss Platt is being very patient with me, and I'm doing extra stuff on my own too. I know I can be a bit dippy and daydreamy at school, but I'm trying hard *not* to be.'

There! I hadn't told a single lie!

Mum rolled her eyes in exasperation (*Is that a word? Think so!*). 'That's precisely what your primary school teachers used to say about you, Jasmin,' she reminded me. 'They were always going on about how scatterbrained you were.'

'You get good marks in some of your other subjects, though,' Gran remarked, still looking a teeny bit unconvinced. 'You don't seem to be struggling in *those* classes.'

'That's because some of my other teachers are much stricter than Miss Platt, and I'm scared of them, so I work harder,' I replied quickly. You know that's true – you've met Mrs Cairns already!

This time it was Gran's turn to sigh and roll her eyes. 'Oh, these young teachers,' she complained. 'They're just too soft on discipline. When I was at school, the teachers were much tougher...'

I nodded, trying to look interested as Gran went off on one. But secretly I was breathing a sigh of relief. I'd managed to wriggle out of *that* pretty successfully. Everything was OK again for the moment.

But only for the moment.

And if I didn't have enough problems, wait until I tell you what Sienna did *next*.

It was break-time at school on Thursday morning. The bell had rung about five minutes ago, but Mr Gordon, our English teacher, had asked me and another student to stay behind and help him put some books away. I'd told Sienna, May and Izzie that I'd see them outside in the playground, but when I made my way over to the wall where we usually hung out, the girls weren't there. They'd left their bags on the wall, though, and I guessed they'd gone to the school shop to buy some snacks.

I don't know what made me do it. Maybe I just wanted to play a joke on Sienna, pure and simple. Maybe there was a *little* bit of wanting to get my own back on her after what she'd done with my history essay. And perhaps I was secretly curious to find out how Sienna would react if *she* was the butt of a joke, for a change...

Anyway, I didn't stop to think about it much. I grabbed Sienna's designer leather bag and tiptoed back towards the school where I stowed it safely out of sight just behind the open door. Then I lurked around there until Sienna, Izzie and May strolled back to the wall. As soon as I saw them, I ducked out of school again and went over to them as if I'd only just arrived.

'Where's my bag?' Sienna was saying with a frown.

'It must be around here *somewhere*,' May replied. 'Maybe it fell over the wall.'

Sienna leaned over the wall to take a look. 'No, not there,' she groaned. 'D'you think someone's nicked it? All my homework from last night's in it. God, that's *all* I need.'

'Don't worry,' Izzie assured her. 'We'll look around the playground for it.'

'That bag cost a fortune too,' Sienna fretted, as Izzie and May began to search the immediate area around the wall. 'Jasmin, did you see anything?' she asked.

'I don't think so,' I replied, turning slightly pink (*told you I was a bad liar!*). Sienna stared at me, then her eyes narrowed suspiciously.

'Do *you* know where it is, Jasmin?' she demanded.

I couldn't help smiling now. I didn't mind being found out so quickly because I'd never intended to keep the joke going *that* long. I didn't want Sienna to get upset.

'Maybe!' I admitted.

Sienna stared at me. At first I thought I saw a flicker of anger in her amazingly blue eyes, but then, to my relief, she started to laugh.

'You little monkey!' She slapped me on the back. 'You really had me going there. Where is it?'

I grinned at her. 'I'll get it.'

'Your turn to buy me a choccie bar now!' Sienna called after me as I ran across the playground towards the school. I popped behind the open door, fully expecting to see Sienna's bag still there.

It wasn't.

A feeling of disbelief flooded through me. *It wasn't possible*. The bag had been there a moment ago, but now it wasn't.

'Hurry up, Jasmin,' Sienna called from across the playground.

'It's gone!' I called back. A cold shiver ran down my spine as I realised I was totally unsure how Sienna would react to this.

'*What!*' Sienna came racing over, Izzie and May at her heels. 'What do you mean? This isn't funny now, Jasmin!'

'It's not a joke,' I explained quickly. 'I hid your bag here behind the door, and now it's gone...'

Sienna shot me an icy look. 'You idiot! Well, you'd better find it – and fast!' she snapped. 'What happens if I have an asthma attack? My inhaler's in that bag.'

'What?' I stared at her, aghast. 'I didn't know you had asthma!'

'Well, now you do,' Sienna said in a tone of contempt. 'And I just hope you're pleased with yourself, Jasmin Sharma. You'd better go and find my bag *right now*.'

'But we're not allowed in school at break-time,' I began. Sienna just gave me a *look*.

'Izzie, go and search our classroom,' Sienna ordered. 'Someone may have put it in there. And May, you ask people in the playground. I'll search the corridors around here, and as for *you* – ' Sienna flicked me a furious glance – 'you can go and check the lost property office.'

Izzie and May ran off at top speed like it was a matter of life and death. And maybe it was, if Sienna really did have asthma. I felt *wretched* as I scuttled off to the lost property office. Why oh why had I had the stupid idea to play a joke on Sienna in the first place? How I wished I could turn the clock back...

I had to persuade one of the school secretaries to open the lost property office for me, as it was only usually open at lunchtimes and after school. She wasn't too pleased either when I was forced to explain that it had all happened because of a joke. But in the end she relented, probably because I was almost in tears. There were piles of gym clothes, umbrellas, odd shoes and a load of other junk in there, but no designer leather bag.

Frantic now, I hurried back to tell Sienna. I was *dreading* it. But as I approached the door that led into the playground again, I saw Mrs Myers, Izzie and May all grouped around Sienna. My heart lurched. Was she having an asthma attack? But then relief surged through me as I saw that Sienna was clutching her bag in her arms.

'Ah, there you are, Jasmin.' Mrs Myers frowned

at me. 'That was a very silly joke to play, wasn't it? I hope you've apologised to Sienna.'

'Sorry, Sienna,' I murmured. How come Mrs Myers had got involved in all of this?

'Now, let's have no more of these silly tricks,' Mrs Myers clucked. 'Off you go outside.'

'Where was it?' I asked as Mrs Myers went off to the staffroom.

Sienna tossed her head dismissively. 'A year 7 girl found it behind the door and gave it to Mrs Myers,' she said coldly. 'No thanks to *you*. And I don't want to speak to you ever again, Jasmin Sharma.'

Sienna marched off into the playground, leaving me shocked and bewildered. She'd accused me of going OTT about the history essay joke, but wasn't she now doing exactly the same thing? I glanced at Izzie and May, and was upset to see that they looked annoyed with me too.

'Look, I didn't mean that to happen,' I said, chewing my lower lip anxiously. 'It *was* just a joke.'

Izzie and May glanced at each other as if neither of them knew what to say.

'Are you coming?' Sienna called. She'd paused and was staring back at Izzie and May. They hesitated for a moment. Then, slowly, they turned away from me and went over to Sienna.

I was so upset, my knees trembled uncontrollably. I stared after them, tears in my eyes. OK, maybe I'd been a bit silly and it *had* been a stupid joke to play on somebody, but I didn't deserve this, did I? Why was Sienna treating me this way? I couldn't even begin to work it out.

And I realised then, with a sudden insight, that Sienna was way too complex a character for me to understand. Yes, she was pretty and funny and sweet and a great laugh. But she was also challenging and unpredictable and spoilt and just a little bit devious. Did she really have asthma? She'd never mentioned it before, and I'd never seen an inhaler in her bag. Had she made it all up just to make me feel worse?

I could see now that Sienna had a dark side. Was that just me being melodramatic again? This time I didn't think so.

My immediate gut instinct was to avoid Sienna from now on. But where did that leave *me*? Izzie and May were still under Sienna's spell, and that meant I'd be without my best friends at school.

The rest of the day was *awful*. Sienna completely ignored me, and Izzie and May did the same. I just didn't know what to do. The only thing I could think of was to talk to the girls tonight at training, and see what they thought about the whole Sienna thing. Maybe they could give me some advice. And the thought of seeing my lovely footie mates was the only thing that kept me going right through to the end of the day.

Dad dropped me off at training that night, and we were a bit late, so I didn't have much time to speak to the other girls before we started. We all wandered outside and grabbed some footballs to kick around while we waited for Ria.

'Ruby won't be here tonight,' Jo-Jo remarked as we passed a ball around between us. 'Her mum told me she's ill.'

Georgie looked alarmed. 'Do you think she'll be well enough to play against the Gazelles on Saturday?' she demanded anxiously.

Jo-Jo shrugged. 'It didn't sound like it.'

Georgie muttered a rude word under her breath. 'I wonder if Hattie will be able to play?' she speculated. Hattie Richards is an occasional sub of ours, but she doesn't always come to the training sessions and sometimes she isn't available for matches. In the past, if we're a player or two short on the day, we've had to nick them from the Under-Twelves team as they've got a slightly bigger squad than us.

'Are you OK, Jas?' Hannah asked me. 'You look a bit down. Is it maths again?'

'Not really,' I began, wondering if I should spill the whole, woeful story of what had happened that day right now. But then I realised that the other girls' attention had suddenly switched elsewhere. They'd spotted Ria coming towards us, along with someone else.

'Wonder who *that* is?' Lauren whispered, nodding her head at the pretty, blue-eyed, blonde-haired girl at Ria's side.

I didn't reply, even though I knew exactly who the girl was.

I was in shock.

It was Sienna Gerard.

CHAPTER SIX

'Hi, Jasmin!' Sienna waved at me like we were best friends. You'd never have guessed from the smile on her face that she'd told me earlier she never wanted to speak to me again. 'Surprise!'

The rest of the team turned to stare at me. Somehow, I managed to pull myself together enough to force a smile.

'Hi, Sienna,' I said in quite a normal voice. The last thing I'd heard, Sienna was going to try out for the school netball team. She'd said *nothing* about being interested in football.

'Oh, you must be Jasmin's friend from Bramfield!'
Grace exclaimed.

Sienna nodded. Her silky blonde hair was tied
back, and she wore a stylish black and white tracksuit
and *extremely* expensive silver football boots.

'Yep, that's me,' she agreed. 'Jasmin's always
talking about the Stars, so I thought I'd come along
and try out for the team. I didn't tell her, though.
I wanted it to be a big surprise.'

Oh, it was. Believe me.

'We're really pleased to have you along, Sienna,'
Ria said with a welcoming smile. 'We're always
looking for new players.'

The rest of the team now crowded around Sienna,
introducing themselves. I hung back, totally unable
to get my head around what was happening. Sienna
had *never* shown any interest in the Stars before
now when I'd mentioned the team. So what was
going on?

'Any mate of Jasmin's is a mate of ours,' I heard
Georgie declare, and I almost laughed, except this
was *so* not funny.

'Have you played much football before, Sienna?'
Ria asked.

Sienna nodded. 'I used to play soccer when we

lived in the States,' she explained. 'That's what they call it over there, of course. Football is American football, which is pretty much just knocking people over and stomping on them, I think!'

Everyone laughed except me. Then I noticed Katy staring at me so I managed to force another smile.

'You don't *mind* me joining the Stars, do you, Jas?' Sienna asked suddenly. 'You've gone very quiet.'

Of course, that meant *everyone* immediately turned to stare at me. Had Sienna said that on purpose? It was impossible to know.

'Don't be daft, Sienna,' I said brightly. 'I was just surprised, that's all. It's good to see you.'

Sienna smiled innocently at me. 'We're going to have a *great* laugh, Jasmin!'

Are we? All I feel like doing at the moment is running away from her as fast as I can.

'What position do you play, Sienna?' Lauren asked.

'Midfield, usually,' Sienna replied. 'But I can play up-front too. I used to score a lot of goals, even from midfield.'

'Fantastic,' Ria commented, looking thrilled. Our team always had problems finding and keeping players because a lot of girls dropped out of football when they got to twelve or thirteen years old. So

I could understand why everyone was pleased that Sienna was joining. But the thought of playing with her in the Stars made my heart sink. She'd be at the training sessions too, twice a week. I'd never get away from her.

My last remaining hope was that Sienna was lying about playing football in the States, and that she would turn out to be completely rubbish. At one time I would have believed anything that Sienna told me, but now I wasn't so sure. I had come to the conclusion that she'd say almost *anything* if it meant she got her own way. Even if Sienna was simply an OK player and Ria used her as a sub, like Hattie Richards, I reckoned I could just about live with that.

We began with the usual warm-up stuff and then moved on to practising dribbling and running with the ball. Almost from the start, though, I could see that Sienna was comfortable with a football at her feet. She obviously *hadn't* been lying about playing a lot of football in America. But why hadn't she mentioned it until now? I puzzled over this for ages as we practised running, stopping and turning with the ball. Ria had organised us into two lines, facing each other, and then one person from each line had to dribble the ball into the centre, bring it to a halt, step to the side, swap balls with the player from the other line and then dribble it back. Guess who was *my* partner in the line opposite?

I dribbled the ball forward and Sienna did the same. I couldn't help staring at her, wondering why on *earth* she hadn't told me that she played football too. I was beginning to realise that Sienna only told you what *she* wanted you to know. Every other bit of information was kept hidden until she decided it was useful to reveal it. But why had Sienna joined the Stars? Was it simply because she wanted to play football, or was there another reason? Something to do with upsetting me?

I was so deep in thought, I forgot that I had to stop the ball and swap over with Sienna. I realised too late that Sienna had already stopped, and I tried to stamp on the ball with my foot but I'd let it run too far in front of me. I gave a gasp as my boot slid off the ball and I tumbled backwards and landed on my bottom.

'Jasmin, are you OK?' Sienna cried, hauling me to my feet. 'You're not supposed to have a rest in the middle of training!'

Everyone laughed, including me, but it took an

effort. I got to my feet, swapped the balls over and headed back to my place in the line.

'God, Jasmin, you look really down,' whispered Lauren, who was next to me. 'When's your gran going home? You really need to have that talk with your parents.'

'I think she's staying for another week or so,' I murmured. I'd completely forgotten about my maths problems for the moment, but obviously the other girls had assumed that was why I wasn't my usual happy self. They didn't know it was because of Sienna, and how could I tell them now? Everyone thought we were great mates...

I felt even more uneasy when we had a mini-match to finish off the training session. Sienna was good. She was fast and she was skilful, although I noticed that a couple of times she kept the ball to herself when it would have been better to pass it. Like she took a shot herself and missed, when Grace, who was on her team, was in a much better position and would definitely have scored. But maybe that was just me being nasty. Sienna really *was* an excellent player, and she'd be a great addition to any team. I just wished she wasn't playing for *mine*.

'Well done, girls,' Ria said as the training session

finished. 'You're all looking really sharp. It's important we don't lose concentration and drop points before the Christmas break. Just keep your minds *off* what Santa's going to bring you, and keep it on football!' She turned to Sienna. 'We have a player out this weekend because of illness, Sienna, so I'd like to put you straight into the team for Saturday's game.'

Sienna looked thrilled. 'Thanks, Ria!' she exclaimed. 'I won't let you down.'

'Ruby usually plays up-front with Grace,' Ria went on, 'So you'll be taking her place.'

Sienna flung her arm around Grace's shoulders. 'You get four goals and I'll get three, Grace,' she said, 'And we'll win seven-nil!'

There were whoops from the other girls.

'Great stuff,' Georgie said with a grin. I could tell she liked Sienna loads already.

Sienna now threw her other arm around *me*. I tried not to stiffen.

'Oh, I can't wait for Saturday,' she declared. 'It's going to be *so* brilliant playing in the same team with you every week, Jasmin.'

'Yes, it'll be fun,' I said as we all trooped off the pitch towards the changing-room.

Well, what else could I say? My life seemed to be getting more complicated by the day. And I had a horrible sinking feeling that things were now way out of my control...

'And eight times seven is fifty-four—'

'No, Jasmin.' Miss Platt clicked her tongue in annoyance. I was already hot all over with embarrassment and nerves, and she wasn't helping. 'Eight times seven is – anyone?'

Izzie put her hand up.

'Fifty-six, Miss.'

Miss Platt nodded. Biting my lip, I wrote fifty-six on the whiteboard. Friday morning maths class was turning into a nightmare. At the beginning of the lesson, Miss Platt had given me my homework back and had been very pleased with me. That had lasted until she asked me to go up to the front of the class and work out a long multiplication problem on the whiteboard.

Ever since Hannah had started "helping" me with my homework, I'd tried to keep my head down in my maths classes, not putting up my hand to answer questions, not volunteering *any* information and generally trying not to let Miss Platt see that I really hadn't improved that much. But I had a feeling that I'd played the *I need more time to work out stuff, and I get all flustered and get things wrong in class* card a little too often. And now Miss Platt was looking rather annoyed with me.

I stumbled on with the sum.

'And nine times seven is sixty-one—'

Miss Platt sighed.

'Jasmin, I simply can't understand why your homework has shown such a huge improvement, and your work in class isn't of an equivalent standard,' she said crisply. 'Unless...' Her eyes narrowed suspiciously. 'Unless you're getting help from someone at home?'

'No, Miss!' I gasped. Which, of course, was true. And I must have convinced Miss Platt because she nodded.

'Then you're relying too heavily on your calculator,' she replied. (*That* was true – and my calculator's name was Hannah!) 'You know we like you to learn the basics, and that means your times tables. You shouldn't be getting a simple sum like nine times seven wrong.'

Suddenly the bell rang for lunch. I almost collapsed with relief.

'Off you go, then, girls,' Miss Platt said. I thought she might ask me to stay behind, but she didn't. I grabbed my bag and scuttled out in about three seconds flat. Sienna, Izzie and May followed.

'Poor Jas.' Sienna linked arms with me as we went off down the corridor. She'd been my best friend ever since training last night. 'Miss Platt is *so* mean to you.'

I shrugged. 'Well, she's right. I *don't* know my times tables. I always get mixed up.'

'So *is* someone else helping you with your homework?' May asked curiously.

Before I could say anything, Sienna turned on her. '*Don't* say stuff like that about Jasmin,' she snapped. 'You're saying she's *cheating.*'

May flushed. 'Sorry, Jasmin,' she muttered.

'*You* wouldn't say things like that about Jasmin, would you, Izzie?' Sienna demanded.

'Of course not,' Izzie assured her, and Sienna linked arms with her too. May was left alone to walk behind us, and I saw her face fall. Sienna was doing her usual thing of being nice to two of us and leaving the other out in the cold. It was how she worked.

I did feel bad, though, because Sienna was right. What I was doing *was* cheating. But it wouldn't be

115

for much longer, I consoled myself. Once Gran left, I would *have* to confess all to my parents. I had *no* idea how they would react. Maybe they'd be so angry, they'd make me leave the Stars any way. But it was something I knew I had to do, or end up as a (really bad) accountant.

I was glad, though, that Sienna didn't know Hannah was helping me out. I had a nasty feeling she *might* try to use that information against me. I'd been really nervous after training last night that one of the girls would mention it while we were getting changed, but luckily they hadn't. I'd already decided to ask them not to say anything about it in front of Sienna when we met up for our Friday evening get-together tonight.

We went out into the playground, and Sienna wrinkled up her nose in disgust when she saw the queue for the dining hall.

'Let's go and get fish and chips,' she suggested.

'Where?' Izzie asked, puzzled.

'Duh!' Sienna rolled her eyes. 'The chippy, of course.'

'But there's no chippy here!' May sounded bewildered. But I'd already guessed what Sienna was up to.

'No, there *isn't*,' Sienna said in a heavily sarcastic tone. 'But there *is* one in Leeson Street.' She strolled over to the side gate. 'Coming?'

Izzie and May looked shocked. We weren't allowed out of school at lunchtime unless we were going home to eat. Only the sixth-formers had permission to leave school premises.

'Well?' Sienna raised her eyebrows.

'I'll come,' May squeaked, sounding petrified. I knew she was only saying it because she desperately wanted to get on Sienna's good side again. Sienna rewarded her with a dazzling smile.

'Me too,' Izzie agreed, obviously not wanting to be left out.

'Jasmin?' Sienna stared at me challengingly. I hesitated, thinking about what would happen if I didn't go. Sienna would be annoyed and she might turn Izzie and May against me. That would leave me without my best mates at school. And what if Sienna decided to try and do the same with Grace, Katy, Hannah, Lauren and Georgie? She could make sure I was left right out in the cold, isolated and alone at school *and* at football. I *had* to keep in with her.

'All right,' I muttered.

'Great!' Sienna exclaimed triumphantly.

I followed Sienna, Izzie and May out of the gate. I was half-expecting to hear a wailing siren go off and the loud, booming voice of Mrs Docherty, the head teacher, yelling, *Stop those girls!* But nothing happened.

I was terrified as we walked down the street. Sienna was bouncing along, chatting merrily, as if she hadn't a care in the world, but I could tell that Izzie and May were just as nervous as I was.

It was only a few minutes walk to Leeson Street, but it felt like hours. I was so stressed, I didn't want anything to eat when we got there either, so I just shared a bag of chips with May. I hardly ate more than four or five, though, as we made our way back to school. I wanted to hurry, but Sienna was dawdling, eating her chips and battered fish so slowly I could have *screamed*.

We were almost back at the school gates when Izzie gave a frightened gasp.

'There's Mrs Horowitz coming out of the car park!' she spluttered.

My heart lurched. Further along the street, Mrs Horowitz's black four-wheel drive was pulling out of the school car park and heading in our direction.

Izzie, May and I made a run for the gate and dived

inside the playground. Sienna didn't even blink. She finished her chips, lobbed the paper into the bin just outside the gate and strolled in.

'She didn't see us, you idiots!' Sienna laughed as the Horror Witch zoomed off down the street. 'Honestly, you three should chill out.'

May and Izzie giggled nervously, but I didn't. I thought I'd sussed Sienna out, but it hadn't made any difference. I was *still* doing what she wanted me to, wasn't I? What would she ask us next? Was she going to keep pushing us to do ever more daring stuff?

I'd already decided it was much safer not to be friends with Sienna at all. But she still had me well and truly entangled in her web, and I had absolutely no idea how to get out of it.

'Got any maths homework this weekend, Jasmin?' Hannah asked me that evening.

It was a chilly but dry November day, so we'd decided to go ahead and have our usual meet-up in the park. We had to go early, though, while it was still reasonably light, as our parents didn't like us being out too long after dark. Lauren hadn't arrived yet, but the rest of us were on our way to the football pitches, swishing through piles of dry, crisp, crimson and gold and orange autumn leaves. Georgie had already grabbed a handful and tried to shove them down my neck, so I was keeping a sharp eye on her!

'Yep, as usual,' I sighed. 'I didn't bring it with me, though. I thought I'd better have a go at it myself first. Miss Platt is getting fed up with me because my homework is brilliant, but I'm useless in class.'

'Oh, Jas,' Grace said sympathetically. 'That was bound to happen, though, wasn't it?'

I nodded. 'I was hoping you guys might help me decide how I'm going to tell my parents when Gran's gone home. I don't know if I ought to let on that Hannah's been helping me out, because it might get her into trouble, too—'

'I'll be fine,' Hannah broke in. 'Don't worry about it, Jas. Honestly.'

'You'll *have* to tell them Hannah's been helping you, won't you?' Katy remarked. I tried not to smile as I saw Georgie wandering along behind her, secretly stuffing leaves into the hood of Katy's padded silver jacket. 'Otherwise, how will you explain to your parents why you've been doing so well?'

'I know,' I agreed. 'Oh, and there's something else, girls. Have any of you – er – said anything about Hannah helping me with maths in front of Sienna?'

The others shook their heads and I felt highly relieved.

'Why don't you want Sienna to know?' Katy asked curiously.

'It's not just Sienna,' I said quickly. 'I haven't told *any* of my friends at school. I just think it's better if not too many people know about it, that's all.'

'We're dead lucky Sienna's joined the Stars,' Georgie remarked, dropping another handful of leaves gently into Katy's hood. 'She's a fab player and a great laugh too.'

'Yes, she seems like a really amazing person,' Hannah added. 'Well, she must be if Jasmin's made friends with her!'

'That's true,' I said, forcing a smile. 'I don't make friends with just *anyone*, you know.' Well, what else could I say?

'It's getting colder, isn't it?' Katy shivered and pulled her hood up. Then she gave a scream as leaves cascaded all over her. The rest of us were in fits of giggles.

'*Georgie!*' Katy squealed. 'I'll kill you!' But she was laughing too.

'I think we should bury Georgie up to her neck in leaves!' I said, bending down to scoop up two big handfuls. Then I ran towards Georgie who gave a shriek as I pelted her with them. The others joined in and for several minutes we charged around chucking leaves at each other until we were all breathless.

'Where's Lauren?' Hannah complained, picking a leaf out of her hair. 'She's late. Do you think she's coming?'

'Here she is now,' Georgie said. 'And look, she's got someone with her. Oh!' Georgie sounded really pleased. 'It's Sienna!'

No!

But it *was* Sienna, wearing a glamorous midnight-blue jacket trimmed with white fake fur which was gorgeous against her silky blonde hair. She looked like a dream. No wonder nobody could resist wanting to be friends with her.

But I'd never felt so down in my life watching Sienna and Lauren chatting away like old mates as they came to join us.

'Hi, Jasmin!' Sienna bounced over and gave me a hug. It took a lot of effort not to push her away. 'I was just out for a walk in the park when I met Lauren.'

'Really?' I replied, secretly thinking I didn't believe a word of it. I hadn't told Sienna that I was meeting the girls tonight, but I guess I must have mentioned sometime before – when I *thought* Sienna and I were friends – that we always met up on Friday evenings in the park. And now here she was. I felt *sick*.

As always, Sienna had immediately become the focus of everyone's attention.'Great to see you, Sienna,' said Hannah, as Lauren tossed the football she was carrying onto the pitch. 'Are you staying to have a kick-around with us?'

'Try and stop me!' Sienna laughed. She ran after the ball which was rolling gently across the grass, and Grace, Georgie, Katy, Hannah and Lauren rushed to join in. I ran after them, but my legs felt like lead. Sienna was charming all my mates, just like I'd thought she would, but where did that leave *me*? At the moment, I felt like the outsider, looking on helplessly as Sienna took *all* my friends away from me, not just Izzie and May, but the others too. And I could *never* be mates with Sienna now, I thought miserably. So what was I going to do? I had no idea.

But as it turned out, I didn't have a choice, any way. Because when I got home, cold and unhappy, everything started kicking off...

Mum and Dad were waiting for me in the living room. And from the looks on their faces, I knew this wasn't going to be good.

'Jasmin, I've just been speaking to Mrs Horowitz on the phone,' Mum told me. 'She and Miss Platt are still concerned about your performance in your maths classes, especially as your homework has improved so much.'

'Mum, I've *explained* about that,' I gabbled, wishing that I'd never started all this stuff with Hannah. It was doing my head in. It wasn't Hannah's fault, it was mine, but it had made everything *so* much worse. 'I need more time to work things out without being under pressure in class. I'm much better working at home.'

'Miss Platt thinks you're relying on your calculator too much, and that you *still* haven't learnt the basics properly,' Dad said, shaking his head. 'We're very disappointed, Jasmin. Your mum and I thought all the extra tuition you've had over the years had sorted that out.'

I was silent. How could I explain that I just didn't seem to be able to remember *anything* to do with numbers? I didn't understand how they worked and I didn't think I ever would.

'Jasmin, we really think you need to start having on-going maths tuition again,' Mum said gently. 'And for that reason, we want you to leave the Stars at the end of this term.'

CHAPTER SEVEN

It was late, but, as you can probably guess, I couldn't sleep. I lay in bed, going over the conversation with my parents in my head.

They hadn't been harsh about telling me I had to give up football to make more time for maths tuition. They'd been surprisingly sympathetic, actually, which made me feel *worse*.

'If your maths improves after a few months' tuition, we're quite happy for you to re-join the Stars next season,' Dad had told me.

'We know how much you love playing football and being with your friends,' Mum added. 'And of course, you'll still be able to see them, even if you're not in the team.'

I'd tried to fight back. I'd used all the old arguments about football keeping me fit, and I'd promised to try harder in maths classes, but even while I was speaking, I could see from the looks on Mum and Dad's faces that they weren't going to change their minds this time. Then Gran, who'd been out, got home and added her voice to Mum and Dad's, so that was that...

I did think about coming right out with everything, like the girls had been telling me to, and confessing that I hated maths, but I was too scared. I thought Mum and Dad would be so mad at me for cheating, they wouldn't listen to anything I said, and they'd probably make me leave the Stars any way. Either way, I was the loser.

And of course, there was a whole other side to the story that no one knew except me.

Sienna.

Would the Stars even *want* me back next season if they had a brilliant player like Sienna waiting to take my place – permanently?

I curled up into a ball under the duvet, trying not to burst into sobs. Not only would Sienna take my place in the team if I wasn't playing any more, I was sure she would also take my place with the other girls. It wouldn't be Katy, Hannah, Georgie, Grace, Lauren and Jasmin any more. It would be Katy, Hannah, Georgie, Grace, Lauren and Sienna. Maybe it *was* best if I left the Stars now any way, because it would be too upsetting to see Sienna effortlessly take over my footie friends, just like she'd done with Izzie and May...

I pulled the duvet up over my head, and this time I started to cry. How had everything suddenly gone so wrong? I just couldn't see a way out of it, and it seemed easiest to give in and do what my parents wanted. I would be leaving the Stars at Christmas, and Sienna would take my place. It was as simple as that.

The changing-room was buzzing next morning. There were three Stars teams playing at home that day, so there was loads of gossip and laughter and teasing going on as we all got changed into our purple kits.

'Come on, you lot!' Sienna yelled, dragging her Stars shirt out of her bag and waving it around her head like a banner. 'Let's get this party started and beat the pants off the Gazelles!'

'Go for it!' Georgie shouted, slapping Sienna on the back.

The others whooped and clapped. I tried to join in, but it was so noisy, no one noticed that I wasn't saying very much. I'd decided not to tell the other girls today that I was leaving as I didn't want to put them off their game. I was going to do it tomorrow when we met up for our usual girlie Sunday.

We were in our favourite corner of the changing-room, but it was a bit cramped now that Sienna had muscled her way in to join us. We'd all seen her arrive in a *huge* silver American car that looked a bit like a tank on wheels, along with her mum. Mrs Gerard was unbelievable. She was the most glam woman I'd *ever* seen, even more stunning than Mrs Bell, Lauren's gorgeous mum. Blonde hair like Sienna's, film star make-up and a red coat and high-heeled black shoes that just shrieked designer.

Ria was waiting for us as we filed out of the changing-room. I'd hung back a little, pretending to be searching for something in my bag, so I didn't have to walk out with Sienna. She'd gone first, linking arms with Grace and confidently predicting how many goals the two of them would score.

'Good luck, girls,' Ria said encouragingly. I'd

asked Mum if she'd tell Ria I was leaving at the end of the game. I couldn't face doing it myself. 'Just take it steady and you'll be fine,' went on Ria. 'The Gazelles aren't a bad team, but remember, they're near the bottom of the table, and you're in second place. There's a reason for that!'

'Don't worry, Ria,' Sienna said with a wink, then added, 'we will exterminate them!' in a dalek-voice.

The rest of the team laughed, but I didn't. The prospect of playing a whole game with Sienna was making me feel completely low.

'Are you all right, Jasmin?' Hannah asked.

'Fine,' I replied breezily.

We headed out onto the pitch. It was still dry and a little warmer than yesterday. The sky was pale blue and the sun was shining. A perfect day for football. But there were hardly any more games left for me to play now. Our last match before Christmas was against the Allington Angels next Saturday. The Angels were third in the league, just three points behind us, and they would be really tough to beat. It would be my last game as a Stars player. Forever? Probably.

As we spread out around the pitch, I heard someone calling Sienna's name. It was her mum.

Tossing her blonde hair back, Sienna strolled over to her.

'Look, darling, your dad sent me a text for you,' Mrs Gerard cooed, holding out her phone which was shiny black and about as thin as a credit-card. A sparkly bracelet on her wrist glittered in the morning sunlight and I just *knew* they were probably *real* diamonds. All the other parents grouped around the touchline, including my mum, were staring in disbelief at Mrs Gerard perched on her sky-high designer shoes. 'Daddy says to make sure you score at least *two* goals.'

Sienna nodded. 'Sure thing,' she said carelessly.

'And if you do, we'll go shopping this afternoon and you can have *whatever* you want,' Mrs Gerard promised.

Sienna waved at her as she ran over to her position on the field. I'd been right when I guessed Sienna was spoilt rotten at home, I thought. Maybe that was why she always wanted to have her own way with everyone else, manipulating people and even telling lies to make sure she got what she wanted—

'*Jasmin!*'

I almost jumped out of my skin as the ball whizzed past me and out of play. I'd been so deep in thought, I hadn't even heard the ref blow the whistle to start the game.

'Wake up, you idiot!' Sienna muttered out of the side of her mouth as she flew past me to take the throw-in. 'We want to win this game, and everyone needs to be up for it, *not* half-asleep.'

God, I was so annoyed, I could have tripped Sienna up as she ran past me! She'd only been in the Stars five minutes, and she was already taking over. The worst thing was, she was right. I *had* to concentrate. Even though I was leaving the Stars very soon, I didn't want to let them down.

As the match got underway, it quickly became obvious that the Gazelles felt they had nothing to lose by having a go at us. To our surprise, before we'd managed to get our act together, the Gazelles had had a couple of weak shots at Georgie's goal, followed by one which hit the crossbar.

'Come *on*, you guys!' Georgie yelled impatiently, gathering the ball safely into her arms as it rebounded into the penalty area. 'Get moving – we haven't even been *near* their goal yet!'

She flung the ball out to Jo-Jo. Jo-Jo passed it quickly to Debs, who side-footed it to Katy. The Gazelles were scampering back upfield – they'd got so involved in their attacking move they'd left huge holes in their defence.

Katy rolled the ball forward for Lauren to latch on to. Lauren was looking for the run up the wing, but a Gazelles defender was on to her, so Lauren whacked the ball over to me instead. Without even thinking about it, I slotted the ball neatly through a gap in the midfield to Sienna who was lurking on the other side of the field.

'Come on, darling!' yelled Sienna's mum. She might be posh, but she was very loud, even louder than Hannah's dad used to be before he stopped himself shouting!

Sienna took off at a storming pace down the opposite wing. The Gazelles defenders just couldn't keep up with her. Sienna cut inside, which they weren't expecting, and then just kept going. Grace was running alongside her into the penalty area and was in a great position to get a shot in, but Sienna wasn't giving the ball up for anyone.

'Pass!' Georgie was roaring from our goal.

I didn't think Sienna would take any notice, but at last she did. She flicked the ball over to Grace who slipped on a patch of muddy grass as she collected it. The whole Stars team groaned, but *somehow*

Grace lunged desperately forward and still managed to get her foot to the ball. It sailed into the net past the outstretched hand of the Gazelles keeper. One-nil!

Everyone applauded. But even above the noise, I could still hear Sienna's mum screaming with delight.

'YES!' Sienna yelled excitedly. She dashed over to Grace and threw her arms around her. 'Didn't I tell you we'd make a great team?'

'You did,' Grace laughed as the rest of us crowded around to congratulate them. 'And you were right.'

'That was a brilliant pass that set Sienna off on her run, Jasmin,' Katy said, patting me on the back. 'Great stuff.'

'Yes, nice one, Jas,' Sienna added. I guess I was the only person who noticed the slightly patronising edge to her voice.

'Let's try to get another goal before half-time,' Lauren said eagerly.

We kicked off again, and this time we looked much stronger as we surged forward. Our goal had knocked the stuffing out of the Gazelles and they were flustered. Even though I didn't like Sienna, I had to admit she was playing like a complete star. She was all over the pitch, one minute helping out in defence, the next racing forward with the blistering pace that the Gazelles defence just couldn't cope with. We had some great chances to go two up – Lauren just clipped the post, and Emily headed wide – but the score stayed at 1-0.

Then, a few minutes before half-time, Hannah dummied the girl who was marking her and then fired the ball at Sienna, who again went running up-field. Grace was already on the edge of the Gazelles penalty area, and was left pretty much clear as the Gazelles defence raced over to stop Sienna.

I thought Sienna would pass to Grace, who was waving frantically at her, but she didn't. Instead she attempted to go around three defenders one after the other, and failed. The third defender stuck her leg out as Sienna tried a shot and the ball ricocheted harmlessly off the field for a goal kick.

'Sorry, Grace,' Sienna called with an apologetic shrug, 'I didn't see you there.'

Yeah, right, I thought. *I wonder how many times she can use THAT excuse.* Sienna was obviously determined to get a goal or two after that text from her dad, and she wasn't bothered if the team suffered because of it.

Maybe I was being a *teeny* bit bitchy, but Ria said

the same thing when we broke for half-time. After praising our commitment and hard work, she turned to Sienna.

'You're playing fantastically well, Sienna, but do try to be aware of what's happening on the pitch around you,' Ria pointed out. 'Don't always assume that you're in the best position to score. Someone else, like Grace, may be better placed.'

I thought I saw a flash of anger in Sienna's blue eyes, but then it was gone. I don't think anyone noticed except me.

'I'll try, Ria,' she said meekly.

When we kicked off for the second half, the Gazelles had re-grouped and were looking more determined. They began defending in numbers, trying to stop us scoring again and hoping for a lucky break so they could pull one back and level the match.

I hated to admit it, but Sienna was *fabulous*. She played even better than she had in the first half, yelling encouragement at everyone and making sweeping runs up and down the pitch. The Gazelles looked totally petrified every time she got the ball. And yet, there were still signs here and there of Sienna being greedy with the ball, and not passing when it would be better for the team. I'd noticed Lauren frowning a few times when she'd yelled for the ball, and Sienna had completely ignored her.

And what about me? Well, I just sort of faded away... Sienna playing so brilliantly made me feel miserable and empty inside. I *know* I should have been pleased for the team, but I couldn't help it. I had no get up and go left in me, and it was an effort to fight for the ball.

Time was ticking away, but we still had our one goal lead. Then Jo-Jo booted a long ball out of defence which fell into the midfield, pretty much at Sienna's feet. She took off on one of her runs, with her mum shouting and cheering like a mad thing from the sidelines.

This time Sienna *did* manage to beat three defenders one after the other. She hooked the ball away from one, dummied another and did a Ronaldo-style step-over to get away from the third. Then she charged into the penalty area and this time there was no stopping her. Sienna let fly a perfect, low shot that wasn't going anywhere except into the corner of the net. And it did.

The Stars went wild. So did Mrs Gerard, who was practically jumping up and down with glee. Sienna was glowing with triumph, and I had to force myself to run over to her with the others to congratulate her. Not because I didn't think it was an amazing individual goal, but because Sienna's brilliance made me feel a thousand times worse about myself. The team wouldn't miss me when I left, I told myself as we all crowded around Sienna. I hated to admit it, but she was a much better player than me.

The Gazelles were looking defeated now and were just waiting for the final whistle which came about five minutes later. As they trooped glumly off the field, the Stars began hugging each other triumphantly.

'Sienna, you were absolutely amazing!' Georgie told her. There were shouts of agreement from the others. I kept quiet until I saw Lauren gazing at me, looking a bit surprised, so hastily I joined in the cheers.

'Oh, I didn't think I was that great,' Sienna said modestly. 'I can play much better than *that*.'

I wondered if she was joking but she looked totally serious. The others were laughing, though.

'Sienna! Over here, darling!'

Mrs Gerard was at it again, yelling her head off. Sienna ran over to her as Katy, Hannah, Alicia, Debs and the rest of the team began to wander over to the changing-room, still fizzing with delight at the victory, even though Ria came over to tell us that the Belles had won their game today too. But I hung back a little, pretending to re-tie my bootlace. I was curious to hear what Sienna's mum was going to say.

'Well done, darling, you were brilliant!' Mrs Gerard gushed. 'I texted Daddy and told him you scored.' Just then her phone beeped.

'Is that a message from him?' Sienna asked eagerly, taking the phone from her mum. She read the text and her face fell. Mrs Gerard squinted at the text too.

'*Just the one goal, Sienna, sweetie?*' she read out. '*I expected you to score two.*'

Sienna scowled. 'Dad's never happy, is he?' she muttered. 'Whatever I do, it's not good enough.'

'Well, I think you were wonderful, darling,' Mrs Gerard declared quickly. 'We'll go shopping when you've changed, and you can choose some new clothes.'

'Whatever,' Sienna muttered, flouncing off.

I followed her to the changing-room. I'm not a psychiatrist or a psychologist or whatever they're called, but even I could see that Sienna had some 'issues' with her parents. A mum who spoilt her rotten, and a dad who seemed to be pushing her to achieve. Maybe that was why she was like she was, I thought, feeling a bit sorry for her. It certainly helped to explain a few things...

'Jasmin?' Ria had gone over to chat to the others as they went into the changing-room, but now she was waiting in the corridor for me. She looked concerned. 'I'm so sorry to hear you're leaving the Stars. Your mum's just told me.'

Ria sounded like she meant it too, even with Sienna around to take my place, and I bit my lip.

'You're a good, solid member of the team, Jasmin, and we'll be sad to lose you,' Ria went on gently. 'Your mum says you might come back, and I want you to know you'll always be welcome. OK?'

'Thanks, Ria,' I said shakily.

Ria patted my arm and went off outside again. Swallowing down an *enormous* lump in my throat, I walked slowly towards the changing-room. I could hear laughter and loud chatter coming from inside as the girls celebrated our victory. I was sure that Sienna was right in the middle of it, and now I really did feel like an outsider. All that was left was for me to tell Georgie, Lauren, Katy, Grace and Hannah that tomorrow I was leaving the team.

But would they even care that I was leaving with Superstar Sienna right there to take my place?

'When you invited us to Sunday lunch, Han, I didn't know *you* were going to be cooking,' Georgie said. She was staring with deep suspicion at the cottage pie Hannah had just proudly placed on the Fleetwoods' dining table.

Katy, Grace and Lauren giggled, but I couldn't manage much of a smile. I was too wound up about having to tell the girls that I was leaving the Stars. And the most upsetting thing was, I had *no* idea how they were going to react.

'Cheeky monkey,' Hannah said indignantly. 'I'll have you know, Georgia Taylor, that I'm quite a good cook.'

Georgie sniffed the steaming dish. 'Smells OK, I guess,' she remarked.

'I'll just get the veggies,' Hannah said, sticking her tongue out at Georgie as she went back to the kitchen.

'Actually, it smells lush, but don't tell her I said so!' Georgie whispered with a wink. 'No broccoli, I hope, Han,' she called.

'And I hate cabbage,' Katy added.

'Oh, me too, *and* peas,' said Grace.

'And I faint if I so much as *see* a carrot,' Lauren remarked with a grin.

'You lot are a pain in the bum!' Hannah groaned, carrying out a tray of peas, carrots, sweetcorn and broccoli. 'I'm glad I'm not your mum.'

'God, Hannah, this all looks disgustingly healthy,' Grace commented as Hannah began to dish up.

'Yeah, whatever happened to good old junk food?' Georgie asked.

'I wanted to make pizzas, but Mum wouldn't let me.' Hannah rolled her eyes as she passed the plates around. 'She said I had to make a proper Sunday lunch or not at all. However...' She grinned widely at us. 'There's a divine sticky toffee apple pudding for dessert!'

'Sounds great,' Georgie replied, digging into the mound of cottage pie on her plate and forking a lump into her mouth. 'Waaah! It's hot!'

This time I burst into giggles as Georgie began panting and flapping her hands in front of her face. Unfortunately I was laughing so hard, I knocked my fork off the table, and I gave a shriek of surprise as it just missed my foot.

'Serves you right for laughing at me!' Georgie said

with a grin. I poked my tongue out at her, and then screamed again as she threw a small piece of broccoli at me and it landed right in my hair! We all howled with laughter.

'Oh, Jasmin, it's *great* to see a smile on your face,' Katy said, beaming at me. 'We haven't seen much of that for the last few weeks.'

'Yes, what's going on, Jas?' asked Lauren.

I sighed. This was as good a time as any.

'Mum and Dad have told me I have to leave the Stars at Christmas.'

There was silence for a few seconds. I glanced at the girls, and they looked totally shocked and upset.

'But, Jasmin, why?' Lauren gasped.

'Is it because of maths again?' Hannah asked.

I nodded. 'Got it in one. Mum and Dad can't understand why my homework is so great and my class work is rubbish. Miss Platt has sussed that I *still* don't know the basics, so I have to have extra tuition.' I heaved another sigh. 'Thanks for helping me out, Han, but it didn't really help at all, if you see what I mean.'

'Jasmin, you *can't* leave,' Georgie exclaimed. 'The Stars just wouldn't be the same without you and your giggle!'

Lauren slid her arm around my shoulders. 'What can we do to help?'

'Nothing.' I shook my head miserably.

'Jasmin, if ever there was a time to have that conversation with your parents about how much you hate maths, it's now,' Grace reminded me. 'You might be able to change their minds.'

I was silent for a moment. I was touched by the fact that the girls didn't want me to leave, but of course, you and I know that there was something else they didn't have a clue about. *Sienna*...

Because of Sienna, I was feeling defeated and demoralised and I'd basically given up. How sad is that? I knew I ought to stand up for myself and tell my parents everything and take whatever punishment they dished out and fight for the future I *really* wanted (which *wasn't* being an accountant). But it all just seemed like too much effort.

'Thanks, guys,' I said. 'But Mum and Dad really want me to improve my maths and I don't want to upset them, so maybe it's for the best...'

Georgie opened her mouth to say something, but just then the doorbell rang.

'Oh, God, I hope this isn't Olivia coming home,' Hannah muttered, sliding off her chair. 'She was supposed to be out all afternoon with her mates.'

'Of *course* it's not for the best, Jasmin,' Lauren said with a frown. 'If you really and truly wanted to become an accountant and join the family firm, then, yep, extra tuition is a great idea. But you *don't*—'

She broke off as Hannah came back into the room. Guess who was behind her.

'Here's Sienna,' Hannah said, looking a bit surprised.

'Oh, hi, guys!' Sienna exclaimed with a huge smile. 'Sorry, am I interrupting something?'

'Of course not,' Georgie replied, raising her eyebrows. 'Sit down and have some of Hannah's mega-tasty cottage pie.'

Sienna didn't need a second invite. She sat down next to Grace and Hannah handed her a plate.

'I just popped round to give you this, Hannah.' Sienna took Hannah's purple scarf out of her bag. 'You left it in the changing-room yesterday.'

'Oh, thanks!' Hannah took the scarf. 'I wondered where it had got to.'

OK, I know I have a really suspicious mind, but I *did* wonder if Sienna had overheard Hannah inviting us to hers today, and had secretly nicked Hannah's scarf to give her an excuse to come round.

'How did you get here, Sienna?' Katy asked. 'Don't you live miles away?'

Sienna nodded. 'My mum dropped me off,' she explained. 'Then I was going to walk into town and mooch around on my own.'

'Well, now you can stay here with us instead,' Hannah told her.

'Fab!' Sienna grinned, looking thrilled. 'If you're sure you don't mind...?'

Was it my imagination, or did she flick me a challenging look?

''Course not,' Grace replied.

At that moment my phone beeped. I took a look and it was just a text from Mum reminding me not to be late home for dinner. But I needed to get away right now.

'Sorry, guys, I've got to go.' I pushed my untouched plate away from me. 'Gran's decided she wants us all to go and visit her sister this afternoon.'

'Oh, shame,' said Katy, giving me a hug. 'But don't worry, Jasmin.'

'Yes, we'll think of *something*,' Georgie added.

'What's going on?' Sienna asked curiously.

I said goodbyes and slipped out of the room. As I put my coat on in the hall, I could hear Georgie explaining to Sienna that I was leaving the Stars because I was getting extra maths tuition, but luckily she said nothing about Hannah helping me out for the last month or so. I just hoped the other girls remembered that I'd asked them not to say anything. Maybe it didn't matter now any way, but I still didn't trust Sienna.

Miserably I let myself out of the Fleetwoods' house and began the walk home, texting Mum to tell her I was on my way.

Everything I thought would happen was coming true. Sienna was taking my place in the Stars and she was also taking my place with my football mates, as well as my school friends. And what could I do to stop her? Nothing. No one would believe me if I tried to tell them what she was really like.

Tears welled up in my eyes and I gulped, feeling lower than I'd ever felt in my whole life. I was well and truly on my own from now on.

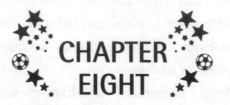

CHAPTER
EIGHT

'Jasmin, I'm *soo* sorry you've got to leave the Stars!' was the first thing Sienna said to me at school on Monday morning. She looked genuinely upset too, but then she *is* a really good actress.

Izzie and May looked shocked.

'What's happened, Jasmin?' asked May.

'Oh, nothing, really,' I said breezily. I did *not* want to give Sienna the satisfaction of seeing that I was upset. 'My parents just want me to spend more time on school work, that's all.'

'That's awful,' May said sympathetically. 'Poor

you. I bet you're gutted, especially as Sienna's just joined.'

I didn't answer *that*.

'How did the match go on Saturday?' Izzie asked.

'Oh, it was OK,' Sienna replied modestly. 'I scored one goal and made another.'

Izzie and May both told her how great she was. I didn't say anything, although I noticed that Sienna never mentioned I'd set her up to help Grace get the first goal.

'The other girls are really upset that you're leaving, Jasmin,' Sienna went on. 'But they were saying that at least they've got me to take your place!'

She laughed. It was a real struggle for me not to react, but somehow I managed it. I'd always been open and upfront about my feelings, and all this trying to hide my emotions was new to me, and I hated it.

'Right, I'd better just dash to the library and return my books before lessons.' Sienna picked up her bag. 'See you later.'

Izzie, May and I were left alone.

'Are you *really* OK about leaving the Stars, Jasmin?' May asked curiously.

'No, of course not.' I sighed. 'But they'll be all right without me. They've got Sienna, and she's a good player.'

'I thought she would be,' May replied. 'Sienna's so confident, I can't imagine her being bad at *anything*.'

There was silence for a moment. I wondered if it was worth making an attempt to find out if Izzie and May genuinely liked Sienna, or if they were nervous of her, like I was.

'Yes,' I said cautiously. 'But I *do* find Sienna a bit full-on at times. Do you?'

I tried to sound casual, but I saw May blush and Izzie couldn't look me in the eye.

'Oh no,' Izzie said firmly. 'Sienna's fab. I love her to bits.'

'Me too,' May agreed.

I gave up there and then. Even if Izzie and May *did* have secret doubts about Sienna, there was no way they were going to confide in me. The hold Sienna had over them was far too strong.

It was a bad day. Sienna seemed determined to keep going on about me leaving the Stars, which totally depressed me, even though I knew she was doing it on purpose. But I did get texts all through the day from Grace, Hannah, Georgie, Katy and

Lauren, telling me not to give up and that they were determined to help me stay in the team. I didn't really see what they could do, but I was pleased all the same.

By the time Tuesday came round, I couldn't decide whether to go to training or not. There didn't seem a lot of point now I was leaving at the end of the week. And Sienna had been unbearable all day, going on about how much she liked the other girls, and how much she was going to enjoy playing with them all. It was *sickening*.

So when Sienna asked me at the end of the school day if I was going to training that night – obviously thinking I'd say "no" – I said, 'Yes. Why not?'

I know it's childish, but I felt quite pleased that I'd wrong-footed her for once!

That feeling soon faded, though, when I was home packing my bag for the training session.

I'll only do this twice more, I thought to myself. *Once at training on Thursday, and then again for the match against the Allington Angels on Saturday. And then that's it. Finished.*

I picked up my bag and went downstairs, when all I really wanted to do was crawl under my duvet and hide away from everyone. I'd always been a happy, bubbly, smiley kind of person, but now it was like Sienna had made me into someone completely different, someone I didn't even recognise as being *me*. How I wished I'd never met her…

'Jasmin, are you all right?' Gran asked with a frown. She was sitting on the sofa, reading, when I went into the living room to find Mum.

'Fine,' I replied automatically.

'You look tired, sweetie.' Gran took off her glasses and peered at my face. 'You've been doing too much lately with all these extra activities. It'll be good for you to take a break from football.'

'Yes, Gran.' It seemed easiest, and much less trouble, not to argue.

Gran was still staring at me, though, and I got the impression she was about to say something else, but just then Mum came in.

'Shall I cook dinner tonight?' Gran offered as Mum picked up her car keys.'

'Oh, it's already prepared,' Mum replied. 'A nice, *healthy* salmon salad.'

Gran pulled a face and went back to her book as Mum and I left the house.

'Jasmin, are you OK?' Mum asked me as we drove to the training ground.

I almost laughed. This was getting ridiculous. 'I'm fine.'

'I know it's a big wrench for you to give up the Stars, darling,' Mum went on. 'But you do see, don't you, that studying is more important right now? This is your future we're talking about, and your dad and I are worried that you won't achieve your true potential if you don't sort yourself out while there's still time.'

I knew she was talking about maths, and my dazzling future as an accountant – *not*. I'd probably be sued by all my clients for getting their accounts wrong, I thought glumly.

We got stuck in a traffic jam in the centre of town because the Mayor was there to switch on the Christmas lights, and there was a big crowd of people gathered in the market square to watch. I'd almost forgotten that Christmas was coming, I thought, as Mum drove past the glittering white snowflakes and jolly Santas perched on lamp-posts. Nothing seemed that interesting and exciting any more now that my whole life had been turned upside-down...

God, Jasmin, get a grip! You're turning into a complete saddo!

By the time I got to the training session, everyone else was already outside. I got changed quickly and ran to join them. They were already warming up by jogging around the pitch, and there, of course, was Sienna, wearing a stunning red tracksuit, her blonde hair knotted on top of her head, running with Grace, Hannah, Lauren, Katy and Georgie. Quietly I joined the back of the crowd and began to jog. I noticed that Ruby was back from her illness and was running alongside Alicia and Debs.

Katy glanced around and saw me. She waved at me to move up and join them. I shook my head. Katy made a pretend-annoyed face at me and then dropped back.

'Hi, Jasmin,' she said. 'You OK?'

'Yep.' This was getting boring now!

I wasn't expecting it but, to my delight, the others noticed where Katy had gone and also dropped back to join us. Sienna followed too, although she didn't look very pleased about it.

'Don't think we've given up on you, Jasmin Sharma,' Lauren said, slapping me on the back, 'because we *haven't*! We're still talking about what we can do to help.'

'Really?' I felt all warm inside that my mates

cared so much – until Sienna went and opened her big mouth.

'Do you think your parents will change their minds, though, Jasmin?' she remarked. 'They seem pretty set on you doing this extra maths stuff.'

'We'll see!' Georgie replied with a wink. I know it was a bit nasty of me, but I was pleased to see a look of irritation flash briefly across Sienna's face. I still didn't see what the others could do to help me, though.

Despite the girls cheering me up a little, it wasn't my best training session by a long, long way. I was having one of my clumsy and awkward days as I tripped over my own feet, the ball and anything else that was nearby. I'm usually quite good at dribbling, but today I stubbed my toe on the edge of one of the cones. I hopped around, holding my foot, which made everyone laugh. Sienna was loudest, I noticed.

Later on, Ria split us up into groups of three to practise ball control and volleying. She told me to work with Katy and Sienna, and that just about finished me off for the night. We had to stand in a triangle shape and pass the ball to each other without letting it touch the ground, using only our feet, though, and not our heads. Ria warned us it was difficult, and she wasn't kidding. I'm not that great at volleying at the best of times, but today I was *rubbish*. Sienna was watching me with a slight smile on her face, which did nothing for my already zero-rated confidence, and, getting more and more flustered, I missed almost every ball that she and Katy passed to me.

'God, Jasmin, you're really not up for it tonight, are you?' Sienna remarked as Katy chased after yet another ball that had gone astray. 'Maybe it's a good thing you're giving up football!'

I tried not to react. But Ruby, who was working alongside us with Debs and Jo-Jo, must have heard because she turned to look at Sienna in surprise.

'Oh, I'm just having an off day,' I replied.

'What's that?' Katy asked, bouncing the ball as she ran back to us.

'Nothing,' Sienna said breezily. 'Let's see if we can keep the ball up in the air for at *least* five seconds, shall we, girls?'

Ria came over to watch and give us some advice, and I tried my best, but nothing was working for me tonight. I might just as well have stayed at home, I thought miserably.

'Right, girls, off you go and get changed,' Ria told us at the end of the session. 'Jasmin, can I have a word with you, please?'

I waited as everyone else went off to the changing-room. Ria was looking a bit uncomfortable, and I wondered why.

Ria cleared her throat. 'You're not OK at the moment, are you, Jasmin?'

Well, at least it was a different way of asking pretty much the same question!

'I'm just gutted about having to leave the Stars, that's all,' I said.

'Mm, that's what I wanted to talk to you about.' Ria looked even more uncomfortable, which worried me. What was she going to say? 'You're not at your best right now, are you?'

'I know,' I admitted. 'Sorry.'

Ria sighed. 'This is really hard, Jasmin, because you're a loyal Stars player. But you know what a good team the Allington Angels are, and now that Ruby's back, I have a bit of a dilemma...'

'Oh?' I said slowly. I was beginning to see where Ria was going with this.

'I now have twelve players to choose from for Saturday's game,' Ria went on. 'And I want to put Ruby back in the team. So, to be perfectly honest, Jasmin, I think that Sienna should play on Saturday against the Angels. Not you.'

CHAPTER NINE

I stared at Ria in shocked silence. I should have seen this coming.

'I feel bad about it, Jasmin,' Ria went on, looking guilty. 'I know it's your last match for us, and I'll definitely put you in as a sub. I *promise* you'll get a decent amount of playing time, even if you don't start the game—'

I was determined *not* to cry.

'Ria, it's fine, honestly,' I broke in. 'You're only thinking about the team, and I haven't been playing that well lately. I understand.'

Ria sighed. 'Are you sure?' she asked. '*Please* don't

pull out of the match on Saturday because of this, will you, Jasmin? The others would never forgive me, and between you and me, I'm a bit scared of Georgie when she gets that manic glint in her eyes!'

I forced a smile.

'I'll be there, Ria,' I promised.

'Thank you.' Ria smiled at me. 'Now off you go and get changed.'

I stood on my own for a few moments after Ria had gone, struggling to hold back the tears before I made my way to the changing-room. Everyone else had already left apart from Georgie, Hannah, Lauren, Katy and Grace. Sienna had gone too, which I was relieved about. The other girls were huddled in a little circle with their heads together, talking in low voices. They turned to look at me when I went in.

'Oh, there you are, Jasmin,' Lauren said. 'What did Ria want?'

I sat down on the bench and began unlacing my boots.

'She told me that I'm only going to be a sub against the Angels,' I replied. 'Sienna's taking my place in the team.'

'*What!*' Georgie exclaimed. 'Ria can't do *that*!'

I shrugged. 'She was really nice about it.' I kicked

my boots off and one sailed across the room and landed on the opposite bench. It was the best shot I'd had all night! 'It's for the team, after all. Sienna' – the name stuck in my throat – 'Sienna's a much better player than me, so it makes sense, especially as I'm leaving.'

'Jasmin, what's happened to you?' Katy asked, concerned. 'You've changed so much over the last few weeks.'

'Yeah, you have,' Georgie agreed. 'You used to be so full of life and up for it.'

'Is it just all this stuff with your parents?' Hannah wanted to know.

'I guess so,' I said, pulling my shirt over my head. How could I tell them about Sienna? They just wouldn't believe me.

'Well, we're not down and out yet, Miss Sharma!' Lauren replied as I threw the shirt into my bag. 'Make sure you're at mine tomorrow after school, 5.30 sharp.'

I stared at her. 'What's going on?'

'Never you mind, nosey!' Lauren said with a grin. 'And wear your Stars shirt.'

'But our parents don't like us meeting up in the week,' I began.

'Just get it sorted and be at Lauren's, like she said,' Grace told me.

I nodded. I didn't know what the girls were planning, but it would be fun to spend some more time with them. Because I knew that when I'd left the Stars, I wouldn't see them nearly so often. Especially if Sienna had anything to do with it.

I waved at Mum as she pulled out of the Bells' drive and then I rang the doorbell. I hadn't been too hopeful that my parents would let me go to Lauren's for tea on a school day, but they'd said yes straight away. I got the impression they were a bit concerned about me and thought I needed cheering up. They were right.

I'd been to Lauren's house loads of times, but I was always amazed by how big and posh it was. Lauren didn't show off about it at all, though. She was such a sweetie, even though she had a temper as bad as Georgie's sometimes. God, I was going to miss them all so much...

I could hear barking inside, and then the door opened. Lauren was standing there in her Stars shirt, clinging onto Chelsea's collar. Chelsea had a purple ribbon tied to it like she always wore for our matches.

'Oh, great, you're here!' Lauren ushered me inside,

and then let go of Chelsea. Chelsea launched herself at me like a missile, licking my hands. 'Come on, we're all in the living room.'

With Chelsea prancing along in front of us, I followed Lauren into the living room – and stopped dead. There were purple balloons everywhere, and a huge, sparkly pink and purple banner was strung along the wall over the sofa. It read *Team Jasmin!* There were sandwiches and cans of Coke on the table, and in the middle was a big sponge cake with words in purple icing which also said *Team Jasmin!*

The other girls, who were all wearing their Stars shirts, jumped up from the sofas as we went in, and then they hugged me to bits, one by one.

'Surprise!' Hannah yelled, beaming.

'Welcome to the Team Jasmin party!' said Katy, giving me a squeeze.

'My mum made the cake,' Grace added. 'Isn't it cool?'

I nodded, so overwhelmed I couldn't say a word.

'Now you sit here and keep quiet, Jasmin,' Georgie ordered, hustling me over to one of the sofas.

I sat down obediently, still too dazed to take it all in.

'Lauren, you first,' Grace told her.

Lauren marched over to stand in the middle of the room.

'OK, I get to go first, because I've known Jasmin the longest,' Lauren began, smiling at me. 'We went to the same primary school. We weren't in the same class so we didn't know each other that well, but I've never forgotten how Jasmin stood up for one of her friends who was getting bullied by the nastiest boy in the school. It was the talk of the playground for *weeks*.'

I remembered that. Martin Carstairs was the bully's name, and I'd told him my brother was a martial arts expert and he'd floor him if he ever bullied me or any of my friends again. Luckily Dan had never been called on to demonstrate his kick-boxing skills, which was lucky because they didn't exist!

'I thought Jasmin was really brave,' Lauren went on, 'and I was *so* pleased when we both joined the Stars. But I've only got to know her well over the last year or so – and you know what? She's even more amazing than I thought she was.'

I felt a bit teary at that, but before I could say anything, Lauren sat down and Georgie bounded into the centre of the room.

'Right, the first time I met Jasmin was when she joined the Stars,' Georgie began. 'She put two goals past me when we played a practice match at her first training session. God, I was *mad*. But then I got my own back when we went out to the car park, and Jasmin stepped in a huge pile of dog poo!'

Everyone laughed and I joined in. I remembered that very clearly. My very first day at the Stars and I'd done everything right up until I was leaving!

'That was *so* Jasmin!' Georgie went on. 'But you know what? She didn't make a fuss and she wasn't all girlie about it. She just burst into giggles and then we all laughed until we cried because no one can hear Jasmin giggle without joining in!'

Ooh, I was coming over all weepy again, but now Grace took the floor.

'The very first time I met Jasmin was, like Georgie, when she joined the Stars,' Grace declared, smiling at me. 'This amazing girl came bouncing into the changing-room, wearing a funky black and white spotted coat – looking a bit like our Dalmatian, Lewis! – bright red leggings, shiny black boots and a crazy red and white striped ribbon in her hair. I thought it was the coolest outfit *ever*!'

I smiled back at Grace as Katy stood up.

'As you know, I only joined the Stars at the beginning of this year,' she said. 'I was feeling nervous and I was late because I missed the bus and I'd forgotten to bring something to tie my hair back with. Jasmin came over to me and gave me a pink hair band and said I could borrow it. I was really grateful, but when I tried to give it back to her at the end of training, she said I could keep it to remind me of my first day with the best team in Melfield!' Katy touched the pink hair band holding her dark hair off her face. 'I still have it, as you can see.'

'OK, my turn!' Hannah jumped up. 'I was last of all of us to join the Stars, and so I've known Jasmin for the shortest time. But I'll *never* forget that time you all slept over at mine, and Jasmin switched the blender on without checking the top was on properly and we got covered in strawberry milkshake!'

We all burst out laughing, even me.

'And then, thanks to Jasmin, *milkshake* became our special word to use when someone goes off on one,' Hannah went on. 'Jasmin, we love you loads, and we don't want you to leave the Stars—'

I was laughing along with the others, but suddenly

I was crying. The girls gathered around me and Lauren handed me a paper napkin.

'Sorry, guys,' I gulped. 'I love you loads too.'

'Well, it's about time you told us what's going on with you and Sienna, then,' Katy said quietly.

My heart jumped.

'Wh-what do you mean?' I stammered.

'Jasmin, we know something's not right,' Grace said. 'You haven't been yourself for *weeks*.'

'And we've all seen how you are around Sienna,' Hannah put in.

'Yesterday Ruby said she'd heard Sienna being mean to you.' Georgie fixed me with that direct stare of hers. 'What's going on, Jasmin?'

Oh, the relief of spilling everything out! I started right at the beginning and told them how Sienna had dazzled Izzie, May and me at first, and how much we'd liked her. And then I explained how I'd gradually begun to realise that Sienna loved manipulating people to do exactly what she wanted, just for the fun of it. I told them how Sienna had never mentioned that she played football and that it had been a real shock to me when she'd joined the Stars. Since then she'd made it pretty clear to me that she was out to take my place in the team *and* with my friends...

The girls listened in silence.

'I did wonder about Sienna right from the start,' Katy said at last. 'I saw your face when she turned up at training that first time, Jasmin. You looked so upset.'

'Yeah, she seemed a bit too perfect, didn't she?' Georgie said thoughtfully. 'I mean, did she really think we'd buy all that stuff about Hannah leaving her scarf behind?'

'I know,' Hannah chimed in. 'When I thought about it later, I actually remembered putting the scarf in my bag. Sienna must have taken it out again.'

'If Sienna wanted to meet up with us on Sunday, why didn't she just ask if she could come along?' Lauren asked.

'That's not how Sienna works, Lauren,' I replied. 'She likes to feel she's one up on everybody all the time. She'd enjoy thinking she had you all fooled.'

'She's a good footballer, but she's too selfish,' Katy said, shaking her head. 'She doesn't always do what's best for the team.'

I heaved a sigh. 'I don't think I'm that good for the team at the moment, either.'

Grace was staring thoughtfully at me. 'Sienna's really knocked your confidence, hasn't she, Jas?'

'I guess so,' I agreed. 'I've been asking myself why I was so stupid to put up with her when I realised I just didn't trust her. And then *everything* seemed to be going wrong at once, and it was all just too much effort...' My voice tailed away.

'Look, us lot are willing to go and see your mum and dad and ask them to let you stay with the Stars,' Georgie said. 'At least until the end of the season.'

I stared at them in disbelief. 'You mean – you want *me* instead of Sienna?'

'Don't be daft!' Lauren scolded. 'Of course we do. Look at that banner up there – it says Team Jasmin, doesn't it? We're right behind you, Jas!'

'But you'll have to stop moping around like a dead duck and fight for your place in the team,' Grace added. 'Are you up for that?'

I thought for a moment. It was almost like I'd woken up from a long sleep, and I could feel energy and confidence flooding through me from top to toe. All at once I could see clearly what I had to do.

'You bet I'm up for it!' I exclaimed. 'And thanks for offering to come and talk to my parents, girls. But that's something I've got to do for myself. Like you all kept saying, I should have done it a long time ago.'

'You mean, you're going to tell them *everything*?' Katy asked, eyes wide.

I nodded. 'The whole deal. How much I've always secretly hated maths. That Hannah's been helping me. That I don't want to be an accountant. *Everything!* I don't know if they'll let me stay in the Stars after this, but I'm going to give it my best shot.'

The girls clapped and whooped and then they all fell on me and we had a big group hug. I knew I was doing absolutely the right thing.

With Team Jasmin behind me, it was time for me to get real and sort out my life!

I really meant it too. I was all fired up to have that conversation with Mum and Dad when I got home from Lauren's that evening. But Mum and Gran were on their own at home because Dad had gone back to the office, so reluctantly I decided I'd have to wait until I could get my parents together.

But next day, everything changed...

'Jasmin!' Sienna was waiting for me by the gates as I arrived at school the following morning. She looked worried and that worried *me*, even though, with the support of the other girls behind me, I'd decided not to allow her to manipulate me any more. 'I'm glad I caught you. I *have* to warn you, you're in big trouble!'

'What?' I stared at her. 'Why?'

'Mrs Horowitz wants to see you,' Sienna explained. 'I had to go into school to hand some work in to Miss Platt, and I overheard her talking to Mrs Horowitz. The Horror Witch said she'd found out that someone else has been doing your maths homework for you, and she's *really* mad about it. Is that true, Jasmin?'

My throat was dry. 'Yes,' I croaked.

'Oh!' Sienna looked surprised. 'Anyway, Mrs Horowitz said she was going to ring your parents right away. Miss Platt saw me then, and asked me to give you a message to go and see them as soon as you get to school.'

I turned as white as a ghost. How on earth had Mrs Horowitz found out? This was the last thing I needed. My parents would *never* forgive me, and they would never believe, either, that I was planning to confess all myself, as soon as I got the chance. I'd be grounded for life and I *definitely* wouldn't be allowed to stay with the Stars.

I did wonder if Sienna was lying, but only briefly.

She hadn't known that Hannah was helping me because I'd asked the others to say nothing about it, and they'd promised. So it *had* to be true.

'OK, I'll go and see the Horror Witch now,' I said.

'Good luck,' Sienna called after me.

It was all too much. And *so* unfair. I'd been planning to sort things out properly and come clean with my parents, and now everything was ruined. I'd been so upbeat yesterday after meeting up with the girls. But now I couldn't cope any longer. It was all over. I was done for.

I walked around the side of the school, out of Sienna's sight. She'd assume that I was going towards the doors that led to Mrs Horowitz's classroom. But I wasn't.

Instead I slipped out of the side gate and out of the playground into the street.

Mrs Horowitz would have phoned my parents by now, and I was going to get into mega-trouble any way. So a bit more would hardly make any difference.

For the first time in my life, I was playing truant.

CHAPTER
TEN

I kept on walking and didn't look back. I'd never done anything like this before – well, except for that time Sienna made us go to the chippy with her – but nothing really mattered now. I just wanted a bit of time on my own to get my head straight before everything fell apart.

I had no idea where I was going, but somehow my feet carried me towards the town centre of their own free will. I felt uncomfortable as I walked along, feeling that I stuck out like a great big flashing beacon in my Bramfield uniform. I was *sure* that everyone who passed me was wondering why I wasn't at school.

It was starting to rain now, which exactly matched my mood, I thought gloomily. If only I could run away somewhere and hide and never come back...

Suddenly I spotted *Mamma Mia's,* our favourite café. Me and the other girls often stopped off there for milkshakes and doughnuts when we were out on a mega-shopping trip.

I went inside.

'A chocolate milkshake and a raspberry cookie, please,' I mumbled to the woman behind the counter, who nodded, staring hard at my uniform. She didn't say anything, but I felt so uncomfortable, I dropped the plate with my cookie on it. It landed on my tray and the cookie shattered into about a million pieces!

'Sorry!' I gasped. Quickly I grabbed my tray and cookie crumbs and fled right to the back of the café. If anyone who knew me went past, they wouldn't see me lurking in a corner.

But unfortunately, someone who knew me very well was already *inside* the café...

I stopped dead, almost spilling my milkshake.

Gran was sitting at the table in the corner. She had a big creamy cappuccino topped with chocolate powder and an outsize, sticky honey and walnut flapjack in front of her.

Our eyes met. Gran and I stared at each other in complete disbelief, the shock on both our faces quickly changing to guilt.

Gran recovered first. I guess stuffing down cakes and creamy coffee when you were supposed to be on a strictly healthy diet wasn't as bad as playing truant.'

Jasmin!' Gran exclaimed. 'Why aren't you at school?'

'I walked out,' I said. I sounded quite calm, which was amazing. 'I couldn't stand it any longer.'

Gran stared at me in complete astonishment. Honestly, her eyes couldn't have opened *any* wider.

'Sit down, Jasmin.' She pulled out a chair and motioned to me. I sat, placing my tray on the table. My knees were trembling and my tummy was churning around like a washing-machine.

'Have you done this before?' Gran asked sternly. I knew she was angry, but she was just about holding it back.

I shook my head. '*Never.*'

'So why today?'

I hesitated. 'It's a long story.'

'And it had better be a good one,' Gran replied, 'Because you are in serious, *serious* trouble, young lady. I don't know what your mum and dad are going to say when they hear about this.'

I felt tears spring to my eyes, but I took a deep breath and fought them back. Crying wouldn't help me now. I had to explain *exactly* how I was feeling and why. No excuses. I thought of Hannah, Lauren and the other girls – Team Jasmin – and how much they'd supported me, and that helped.

'It all started with maths,' I began, and I saw Gran's eyebrows almost shoot off the top of her head in surprise. 'You and Mum and Dad don't know it, but I hate maths.' *There! I'd said it!* 'I've always hated it...'

I expected Gran to interrupt me then, but she didn't. However, she didn't take her eyes off me once as I explained how over the years I'd struggled and struggled to understand stuff, and how it just never made sense and always seemed to slip right away out of my head again. I told her how much I loved English and drama and art and anything creative, and how maths was just a senseless jumble of facts and figures to me. But the rest of the family simply didn't understand, and thought I was just slacking in class. And then, taking another deep breath, I told her about Hannah "helping" me with my maths homework...

Gran did interrupt me, then, looking furious.

'Jasmin, you've been cheating!' she exclaimed crossly. 'How *could* you be so stupid?'

'I know,' I sighed. 'I've realised that since, believe me. But Mum and Dad were making noises about me leaving the Stars if I needed extra maths tuition and I just *couldn't* face it.'

Gran tutted loudly.

'I didn't let Hannah help me just because I wanted to stay with the Stars,' I said, desperate to explain. 'It was because I didn't want to let Mum and Dad down. I wanted them to be proud of me.'

'And do you think they'll be proud of you when they find out what's been going on?'

I flushed. 'No,' I muttered. 'But don't blame Hannah. She was only trying to help. All the girls kept saying I should talk to Mum and Dad and tell them the truth.'

Gran looked surprised. 'Really?'

I nodded, swallowing hard.

'Yes, they've started calling themselves Team Jasmin because they want to help me stay with the

Stars,' I said. 'But I was just too nervous to have it out with Mum and Dad. I know they want me to become an accountant and join the family firm. They just won't accept that I'm no good at maths. They think I'm lazy.'

Gran was silent for a moment.

'Jasmin, have you ever heard the saying, *There's none so blind as those who will not see?*'

I shook my head.

'Your parents aren't as blind as they seem,' Gran went on. 'Your mum in particular is becoming concerned that maths "just isn't your thing", to use her own words.'

My mouth fell open. 'You're joking!'

'She's discussed it with me and your dad a few times,' Gran explained. 'But your dad insisted that you *had* to be good at maths because it runs in the family, and that you just weren't working hard enough.' She shrugged. 'You're right about one thing, though. He's very set on all of you joining the family firm, and I think that means he doesn't even want to consider the possibility that what your mum's saying might be true.'

For a moment I felt very angry that my parents had suspected I was genuinely struggling. They'd buried their heads in the sand, hoping that I'd suddenly become a maths genius like everyone else. But just as quickly, the anger faded. After all, this was *my* fault too. If I'd told my mum how I was feeling when the other girls had urged me to, it would just have confirmed what she'd been thinking, and then I might never have got into this mess.

'I know you can't understand why I hate maths, Gran,' I mumbled. 'But I do – and I *don't* want to be an accountant.'

'I *can* understand that, actually, Jasmin.' Gran took a sip of cappuccino. 'Because I didn't want to be one either!'

I stared at her in disbelief.

'When I was a little younger than you, I enjoyed maths, but I loved history even more,' Gran explained. 'I wanted to be an archaeologist, but my parents weren't having any of it. They insisted that I had to work harder at maths, so I did – and I found out I was even better at it than I thought I was, and so, in the end, I *did* become an accountant. And I do really enjoy it.' Gran looked a bit embarrassed. 'I suppose I thought it might turn out to be the same for *you*, so I backed your dad up against your mum.

I thought it was a good idea for you to give up football and have more time for extra maths tuition so that you could follow in the rest of the family's footsteps. But to be honest, it doesn't sound like it's going to work.'

'No,' I replied sadly. 'And now Mum and Dad are going to be *really* mad at me.'

'Which reminds me,' Gran said with a frown, '*I'm* really mad at you myself! What on earth were you thinking of, playing truant like this, Jasmin? You still haven't explained yourself properly.'

I realised then that I hadn't told Gran about Sienna. So I dived straight into *that* part of the story. Soon Gran was hanging on my every word as I told her how Sienna seemed to have taken over my life, at school and at football, finally rounding it off by explaining all the stuff with the Horror Witch that Sienna said had happened earlier this morning.

'And I was just *gutted* because there I was, about to confess all to Mum and Dad, and now it's too late because the Horror – er – Mrs Horowitz will have rung them by now,' I concluded sadly.

Gran patted my hand. 'You've really been miserable these last few weeks, haven't you?' she said. I nodded, my bottom lip wobbling. 'Are you sure Sienna wasn't lying about Mrs Horowitz finding out about you and Hannah? She sounds quite a devious little madam.'

'I don't think so, because I asked the other girls not to say anything,' I replied. 'So how could Sienna have known?'

'Maybe one of them let it slip,' Gran suggested.

'No, I don't think so – OH!' I'd suddenly remembered when I'd asked the other girls not to tell Sienna, that Lauren hadn't been there. In fact, that was the Friday evening when Lauren had turned up with Sienna a few moments later. Maybe Lauren had mentioned it to Sienna before they joined us, and *that* was how Sienna knew. It was certainly a possibility.

'Actually, she *might* have known about it,' I admitted. 'Do you think she went and told Mrs Horowitz and Miss Platt herself?'

'Maybe, maybe not.' Gran looked thoughtful. 'I think we should find out. And I also think it's about time I joined Team Jasmin myself!' She opened her purse and handed me a five pound note. 'Go and get me another cappuccino, sweetie. I'm going to ring the school and I *may* have to tell a few fibs, so it's better if you're not listening!'

I gave Gran my phone as it had the school's number in it, then I went over to the counter. I was feeling a little happier because of what Gran had said, but not much. A big, horrible scene with my parents was undoubtedly looming later today.

When the cappuccino was ready, I carried it back to the table to find Gran just putting her phone away.

'OK, all sorted,' Gran said briskly. 'An emergency appointment with the dentist has covered you for today, but your parents will have to email the school to confirm—'

'They won't do that!' I exclaimed.

Gran ignored me. 'Anyway, I made an excuse to speak to Miss Platt to ask if there was any maths homework for you as you were absent today, and I'm absolutely certain that Sienna was lying and that Mrs Horowitz and Miss Platt don't know *anything*. That conversation Sienna said she overheard just didn't happen. And she obviously hasn't said anything to them, either.'

My shoulders sagged with relief. Typical Sienna. She probably just wanted to wind me up by making me think my secret had been discovered. Or maybe she'd hoped I'd go straight to the Horror Witch and give the game away myself! I knew that I had to face up to Sienna and make it clear I didn't want to be friends with her any more. But I still had to face my parents too, and *that* was what was worrying me more.

'Jasmin, you've been a very silly girl,' Gran said, but in a gentler tone than I was expecting. 'But I can see *why* you've done the things you have. You didn't want to disappoint your parents, and that's a good thing. But now it's time for everyone to face up to a few home truths. I'm going to take you home and then get your mum and dad to come back from the office so that we can sort this out right away.'

I gulped. 'OK, Gran.' I knew I might as well get this over with.

'And now, are you going to eat that smashed-up raspberry cookie or not?' Gran pointed at my plate. 'Because if not...'

I handed her the biggest bit. 'Thanks, Gran,' I said. 'And I promise I won't tell Mum and Dad you've been eating and drinking all the things you shouldn't!'

Gran shook her finger at me. 'Frankly, Jasmin, I don't think they're going to care about what I've been doing. Not when they hear what *you've* been up to...'

I sighed. Gran was right. One way or another, everything depended on what my parents decided to do – my whole future, including whether I would ever play for the Stars again.

Heart thumping like crazy, I lay on my bed, listening to the rise and fall of voices coming from the living room downstairs. When we'd got home earlier, Gran had completely surprised me.

'You go up to your room, Jasmin. I think I'd better talk to your mum and dad alone, first.'

The enormous relief I felt must have shown in my face because Gran put her arm around me.

'Don't worry,' she went on. 'Like I said, it's time this was all sorted out. It's gone on far too long.'

'Thanks, Gran,' I'd said shakily. 'I love you for this.'

Gran shook her head at me, but I knew she was pleased. 'Off you go. And try not to worry.'

Easy to say. I sat on my bed and heard Gran pick up the phone in the hall. I couldn't hear what she said, but I knew she was asking my parents to come home right away.

About half an hour later I heard Dad's car pull onto the drive, and then the front door opened.

I heard voices – Gran's, Mum's and Dad's – in the hall, and then they all went into the living room.

I glanced at the clock for the millionth time. They'd been talking for about twenty minutes, and I could hardly bear the suspense. My stomach was tied in knots, and I could hardly breathe. *What was going on down there?*

Then I heard Dad's voice calling me from the living room.

'Jasmin, come down, please.'

I climbed off the bed, my knees trembling uncontrollably, and went downstairs. *Oh, God, this was it...*

They were waiting for me. Gran was on the sofa next to Mum, who looked as if she'd been crying. I felt a rush of guilt. Dad, meanwhile, was pacing up and down the room, looking angry. My heart sank.

'Well, what have you got to say for yourself, young lady?' Mum asked in a clipped voice. 'Your gran's just told us everything. And we're *very* disappointed in you—'

'Sorry!' I blurted out. Tears began to roll down my cheeks. 'I just didn't want to let you down, I know you're disappointed and – and I *hate* myself for it!'

'Oh, Jasmin...' Mum's voice softened just a little. She glanced at Dad, waiting for him to say something. But Dad just shook his head. He still looked angry and didn't seem able to trust himself to speak.

'There are lots of different issues here,' Gran said quietly. 'Yes, Jasmin shouldn't have got help with her maths homework and she shouldn't have played truant from school today. But she didn't do these things because she's a bad girl or because she's lazy. She's just been trying desperately to live up to what you want her to be, and it all got too much for her.'

'Jasmin should have come and talked to us about it, then!' Dad said crossly. I bit my lip. 'How do you think we feel, knowing our daughter is sneaking around behind our backs, getting her friends to do her homework and playing truant from school?'

I hung my head.

'Is it true what Gran told us, Jasmin?' Mum asked. 'Do you really hate maths that much?'

I nodded. 'It makes my head ache,' I replied. 'Even if I understand it one minute, I've forgotten it all again by the next day.'

'But you've been doing OK up until this year,' Mum pointed out.

'That was only because I had the extra tuition from Mrs Rehman when I was at primary school,' I said. 'And even then I could barely keep up.'

'I was beginning to think that was the case,' Mum murmured under her breath.

There was silence for a few moments. Then Mum turned to Dad.

'Raj, this is partly our fault,' she began, 'I can see that now—'

'Nonsense!' Dad retorted. 'All we were trying to do was give our daughter a good start for her future.'

'But I don't have *any* say in my own future at all!' I blurted out. 'I've been really miserable because I don't *want* to be an accountant!'

Dad stared at me in disbelief.

'I know I messed up, but I just didn't want to let you and Mum down,' I explained shakily. 'I know how proud you are of Shanti, Kallie and Dan because they're so good at maths, and I wanted you to feel the same about *me*, instead of just thinking I'm the odd one out—'

Dad's face changed. Suddenly he looked a little guilty. 'Do you think we're *not* proud of you, Jasmin?' he asked.

'Well...' I bit my lip. 'I don't know.'

'Jasmin, how can you think such a thing!' Mum exclaimed in a shocked voice. 'You're gorgeous – pretty, funny and delightful. I wouldn't change you for anything.'

'Except you wish I was good at maths,' I sighed.

'Like I said before, I think this is partly mine and your dad's fault.' Mum stared hard at Dad as if she was willing him to agree. 'I think we got a bit carried away with the new firm being such a success, and wanting it to be a family thing. We'd noticed you weren't happy, Jasmin, but we thought everything would be all right in the end.'

I felt a teeny bit happier, but I wished that Dad would say something. Mum, Gran and I waited.

'I'm still very unhappy about how you went about this, Jasmin,' Dad said quietly. 'And it's a lot to come to terms with all at once. But believe me, if you ever, *ever* get anyone else to do your homework for you *or* leave school without permission again, you won't be allowed out of this house until you're thirty. As it is, you'll be doing extra chores for the next couple of months, at least.'

'I'm so sorry, Dad,' I said tearfully.

Dad came over to me. 'Do you really hate maths

that much?' he asked. 'And you *definitely* don't want to be an accountant?'

I nodded, unable to speak. Dad cleared his throat, but before he could say anything, Mum shot him a pleading glance.

'Well, maybe it'll be useful to have someone creative in the family, after all,' Dad said, trying to force a smile. 'After all, we'll need someone to design all our logos and letterheads and things like that.'

With a sob of relief, I leapt up and threw my arms around him. 'Thanks, Dad!'

'But whatever you decide to do when you leave school, you still need to get your maths GCSE,' Dad warned, hugging me back. 'So no slacking, just because you don't have to become an accountant.'

'And that means you'll probably still have to have extra tuition,' Mum added.

'I won't let you down,' I promised with a huge smile. 'Even if I only get a C, I'll make sure I pass.'

'And what about the Stars?' Gran said.

Mum and Dad looked at each other. I could see from the look on Dad's face what he was going to say, so I jumped in first.

'*Please* don't make me leave,' I begged. 'I know

Hannah shouldn't have helped me with my homework, but the girls kept trying to make me tell you how I felt, and I just chickened out of it. I love them all to bits and I love playing football and I *promise* if you'll let me stay, I'll work *really* hard on my maths and pass my GCSE!'

'I think she means it,' Gran commented.

Dad raised his eyebrows. 'I thought you were keen for Jasmin to give up football?'

'I was,' Gran replied. 'I've changed my mind.' She grinned at me. 'I think Jasmin deserves a second chance. She's been through a lot recently.'

'But what about this rather unpleasant girl, Sienna Gerard?' Mum asked. 'Your gran's told us all about *her*. I thought she'd taken your place in the team?'

'She has,' I replied. 'But I'm going to fight to get it back. If you'll let me.'

'Spoken like a true Sharma.' Dad *did* actually sound quite proud of me. I waited, heart in my mouth. 'All right, Jasmin,' he said at last. 'You can stay with the Stars—'

'Thanks, Dad!' I yelled, launching myself at him again. I could hardly believe it!

'But if your school work suffers in *any* way, you'll

be leaving again,' Dad told me sternly. I could see, though, that he was trying not to smile as I danced madly around the room. 'Understood?'

'Understood!' I gasped. I flung myself at Mum and then Gran for big, sloppy kisses and then I raced upstairs and grabbed my phone to send the same text to Hannah, Lauren, Grace, Georgie and Katy.

All sorted! Had a disaster of a day, but mum and dad r brilliant and they said I can stay with Stars!!! HURRAH!!!

A moment or two later, texts were whizzing back and forwards between me and the girls as we celebrated my return to the best team in Melfield!

Jasmin Sharma was back with a vengeance! And Sienna Gerard had better watch out!

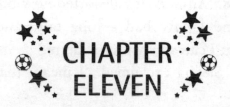

CHAPTER ELEVEN

'What happened to you this morning, Jasmin?' Sienna asked curiously when I went into the playground that afternoon after lunch. Mum had given me a lift back to school so that I wouldn't miss any more lessons. Sienna was with Izzie and May, looking as innocent as if butter wouldn't melt in her mouth. But I was on to her now!

'I forgot I had a dentist's appointment,' I fibbed. 'So I had to leave to meet my gran in town.' Then I went straight on the attack. 'Why did you say all that stuff about Mrs Horowitz and Miss Platt this morning, Sienna? It wasn't true, was it?'

Sienna yawned. 'Chill out, Jasmin, it was just a *joke*.'

'What's going on?' Izzie asked, looking confused. 'What's Sienna been saying?'

'Oh, that Mrs Horowitz had found out someone was helping me with my maths homework,' I explained. 'Anyway, it's all sorted now because my parents and I have had a long talk, and they've agreed that I can stay with the Stars.'

'*What!*' Sienna exclaimed. 'I mean, that's great, Jasmin.'

I smiled, knowing I'd just *really* annoyed her, ha ha.

'Who's been helping you with your maths, then?' Izzie persisted, still looking bewildered. 'And how did Sienna know?'

Sienna turned on her.

'Oh, for God's sake, Izzie!' she snapped. 'Didn't you hear Jasmin say it's all sorted? Just shut up about it!'

Looking hurt, Izzie did shut up. I knew Sienna didn't want me to go into details because that would have made her look really bad.

'I'm going to the library.' Sienna linked arms with me, and then smiled at May. 'Are you two coming?'

She was doing her usual thing of divide and rule, making Izzie feel bad. Well, this time I was ready for her!

'I don't think so,' I said coolly, pulling my arm free. 'I'm going to stay here and chat to Izzie. You were a bit mean to her just now, Sienna.'

There was an electric silence. Izzie and May looked shocked, and I realised this was the first time ever that one of us had refused to do what Sienna wanted. Sienna was looking quite shocked herself, but she quickly pulled herself together.

'Oh, OK, Miss Goody Two Shoes,' she said in a sarcastic voice. 'Come on then, May.'

May hesitated. I stared at her, absolutely *willing* her not to do what Sienna wanted.

'I think I'll stay here with Izzie and Jasmin, actually,' May squeaked, looking terrified.

Sienna gave an unpleasant laugh. 'God, you three are a bunch of losers,' she sneered. 'See you around, then.' And she walked off. It was as easy as that.

'Jasmin, you're so brave!' Izzie threw her arms around me. 'Thanks for standing up for me.'

'No problem,' I said, my confidence soaring. 'I should have done it ages ago.'

'We should *all* have done it,' May chimed in. 'The

times I've wished we'd never made friends with Sienna in the first place!'

'Really?' I asked.

May nodded. 'I guess I was just a tiny bit scared of her,' she admitted, flushing with embarrassment. 'Sienna's just so—'

'Unpredictable?' I suggested.

'Exactly!' May agreed.

'Well, I was a bit scared of her too,' Izzie confessed. 'I *did* like her loads in the beginning, but then I began to think she was spoilt and spiteful. I just didn't know how to get away from her, though.'

'So it's just us three again, like the old days!' I said, sighing with relief. 'Unless Sienna tries to make friends with us again, I guess.'

But Sienna didn't. She ignored us very obviously for the whole afternoon, and began hanging out with Melissa Grey and the rest of the Prom Queens. I didn't care at first, but then I *did* start to wonder what would happen at training that evening and at the match against the Allington Angels on Saturday. What if Sienna ignored me? That wouldn't be good for the team, I fretted...

When Mum dropped me off at the college for training that night, Georgie, Hannah, Lauren, Katy and Grace were all waiting for me on the steps.

They began squealing and waving and jumping up and down like mad things as Mum drew the car to a halt.

'I think your friends are quite pleased you're not leaving the Stars!' Mum remarked as I grabbed my bag from the back seat.

'Thanks, Mum.' I gave her a smacking kiss on the cheek. 'I'm so glad we sorted everything out.'

Mum smiled. 'Me too. Now get out of here before your friends burst with excitement!'

I jumped out of the car and was immediately swamped by a crowd of five cheering girls hugging me from all sides.

'See, we told you Team Jasmin would help!' Georgie yelled, punching me on the shoulder.

'You sure did,' I assured her. 'You gave me my confidence back!'

'And we're *never* letting you leave the team again!' Lauren shrieked as she and Hannah hung onto my arms.

'Don't worry, I'm not going anywhere,' I assured her. 'The Stars is where I belong.'

'So what happened to change your mum and dad's minds?' Katy asked eagerly.

'Yes, tell us all!' Grace added.

As we made our way to the changing-room, I filled the girls in on all the details they didn't know yet – Sienna's lies about Mrs Horowitz, walking out of school and meeting Gran in the café, the difficult conversation with my parents, and then what had happened with Sienna this morning.

'Wow!' Hannah's eyes couldn't be any rounder. 'God, what a shock when you went into *Mamma Mia's* and saw your gran there!'

'It was,' I admitted. 'But it was the best thing that could ever have happened.'

'That's brilliant, Jasmin,' Grace said, slinging her arm around me. 'I'm so glad you're happy again, and that everything is back to normal.'

Georgie frowned. 'Is it, though?'

We all stared at her in surprise.

'Well, what about Sienna?' Georgie went on.

'I'm going to do my best to win my place in the team back from her,' I declared.

'Yes, but we've got to play with her in the meantime,' Georgie pointed out, pulling a face. 'And frankly, I'd rather not be in the same team as *her*.'

'Me too,' said Hannah and Lauren together.

'Look, let's just wait and see what happens,' I said,

wondering if Sienna would even turn up tonight.

'Jasmin!' I heard Ria calling me just as we reached the changing-room. I spun round and beamed at her.

'I'm so glad you're staying with the Stars, Jasmin.' Ria really *did* look pleased. 'Welcome back.'

'Thanks,' I said. 'And I'm going to try to win my place back from Sienna!'

Ria laughed. 'A bit of competition for places is always good for a team,' she replied. 'Great to have you onboard again.'

I skipped into the changing-room on a high. Not even Sienna would be able to bring me down now! Ruby, Jo-Jo and the rest of the team arrived over the next fifteen minutes, but there was still no sign of Sienna. I'd finished changing into my kit and was just tying my hair back when we heard footsteps down the corridor outside.

A few seconds later, Sienna bounced in. 'Hi, girls,' she called as if nothing had happened. But she didn't come over to our corner to get changed. Instead she strolled over and began chatting to Debs and Emily.

'She's got a nerve!' Georgie muttered.

'Chill, Georgie,' I whispered. 'If Sienna's going to be friendly, we can handle it for the sake of the Stars, can't we?'

Georgie pulled another gruesome face, but nodded. And in fact, Sienna was perfectly well-behaved and pleasant during the whole of the training session. She didn't speak to us unless she had to, but there was no drama or anything. She just got on with it, and I was extremely relieved.

I actually remember sighing with relief that the whole thing was now over.

Well, I hoped so, any way.

The match against the Allington Angels on Saturday morning was an away game, and I got a lift with Georgie and her dad to the secondary school where the Allington teams played their matches. We were a bit late because of the Christmas shopping traffic, but as soon as we pulled into the school car park, Ria came rushing to meet us.

'Jasmin, thank goodness you're here!' she exclaimed. 'I've just had a call from Debs' mum. Debs has caught Ruby's cold and can't play today, so we're a girl short. You're back in the team!'

'Great stuff!' I gasped as Georgie hollered with glee. 'Oops, I mean, I'm *really* sorry Debs is ill, but—'

'It's OK, Jasmin,' Ria laughed, 'I know what you mean!'

Quickly we followed Ria to the away team's changing-room to join the rest of the Stars.

'Isn't it fab, Jasmin?' Lauren called, wriggling into her shorts. 'I'm sorry for Debs, but it's so good to have you back.'

'Debs said to go for it, Jasmin!' Ruby told me. 'I just texted her, and she's really pleased you're taking her place.'

I grinned at her. 'Tell Debs I hope she feels better soon.'

'Hurry up and get changed, you two.' Grace glanced at the clock on the wall. 'We're running late.'

'I'm nervous,' Hannah groaned. 'I need the loo.'

'That's the third time in the last five minutes!' Katy pointed out as Hannah hurried off.

'I know, but the Angels are *such* a good team and we *have* to beat them to keep up with the Belles,' Hannah called from the toilet cubicle.

'Does anyone think the Burnlee Bees will beat the Belles today?' Georgie asked.

'No chance,' Grace said with a shrug.

Then something struck me. I glanced around the changing-room.

'Where's Sienna?'

'She's not here yet,' Lauren said anxiously.

'She probably got caught in the traffic, like we did.' Georgie pulled her Stars shirt over her head. 'She'll be here in a minute.'

But would she?

A cold, shivery feeling was running down the length of my spine. I was suddenly wondering if Sienna was going to turn up *at all*.

Would this be her revenge? To leave the Stars playing the Allington Angels with a team of only ten girls? That would be *just* like Sienna.

CHAPTER TWELVE

'Where's Sienna, Ria?' Georgie demanded as we left the changing-room. Kick-off was only a few minutes away.

'I have no idea.' Ria was looking extremely harassed. 'I've rung her and her mum, and I just keep getting voicemail messages.'

'But what are we going to do?' Jo-Jo asked anxiously. The Angels were already taking up their positions on the pitch and the ref was looking at his watch.

'You know the rules,' Ria said with a sigh. 'Either we play with ten girls, or we pull out.'

'Pull out!' Georgie exclaimed. 'No way!'

'We'd better take a vote on it.' Ria looked at us 'Who wants to play?'

Every hand shot up.

'Right, I need to make sure it's OK with the Angels manager and the ref.' Ria hurried off.

'Ask the Angels if they'll play with ten people, too,' Georgie called after her. We knew that was within the rules. But it was up to the Angels whether they agreed or not.

''Course they won't.' Lauren gave Georgie a nudge in the ribs. 'Would *you*, if you were them?'

'I guess not,' Georgie groaned. 'God, this is the *pits*! What the hell's happened to Sienna?'

I guess my face must have showed what I was thinking, because Georgie pounced on me immediately.

'What is it, Jasmin?'

'It's a bit mean,' I began hesitantly, 'but I was wondering if Sienna hasn't turned up on purpose.'

'Sounds just like the sort of thing she'd do,' Hannah said glumly.

'You're kidding, right?' Ruby exclaimed in disbelief. I shook my head.

'We're done for,' Alicia sighed. 'We'll never beat the Angels with just ten of us.'

'Look, don't give up now!' I told them. 'If we do that, and Sienna *is* trying to freak us out, then she's won.'

'Jasmin's right.' Grace backed me up. 'We'll just have to keep it tight at the back and look for a break whenever we can. I'm up for it!'

There were nods all round as Ria came back.

'OK, the Angels have agreed to carry on with the match, but they won't reduce their own team,' she told us. 'So it's ten against eleven. You know what you have to do, girls—'

'Keep it tight at the back, and look for a break!' we chorused.

Ria smiled. 'Good luck. You can only do your best.'

We fanned out across the pitch, taking up our positions. I wondered for a moment whether Sienna would turn up at the very last minute, but then I put her right out of my head as the ref finally blew his whistle. This was a game that needed one hundred per cent concentration if the Stars were going to get anything out of it at all.

The Angels had already realised that this was a great chance for them to thrash the pants off us, and they strung together five attacks in as many minutes. Three fizzled out into nothing, thanks to determined defending by Katy and Jo-Jo, but Georgie had to make one spectacular save and tip another shot around the post.

Our main aim for the first half was just to stop the Angels from scoring. We were all running back up the pitch to defend like mad things, even Grace, who usually stayed around the centre circle. With nine of us back, plus Georgie in goal, the Angels were finding it tough to break us down. And because the Stars had a great team spirit, we weren't going to be a push-over, even with only ten players.

The problem, though, was that when we got the ball out of our goalmouth, we all had to charge up-field again because there was no one ahead of us to pass to! As one of the Angels won the ball back from Lauren in the centre circle and all the Stars chased back to defend again, I wondered just how long we could carry on like this. We were going to be exhausted by the second half.

But somehow, for most of the first half, we managed to keep the score at 0-0. But pretty much all we were doing was standing in front of our goal in numbers to stop the Angels from scoring. Amazingly enough, though, it was working!

And I could see signs that the Angels were getting frustrated. They were starting to get that air of desperation which meant that they were thinking, *There's only ten of them and there's eleven of us, so why haven't we scored yet?* I'd seen it several times in Premiership matches on TV when a player had been sent off. The team with eleven players *didn't* always win, I told myself with rising confidence.

And then, out of the blue...

Georgie had gathered up the ball in her penalty area after yet another attack from the Angels, and was hanging on to it, giving us time to race up the field again so that we could go on the attack. She rolled the ball out to Katy who passed to Alicia. Alicia immediately booted the ball up the field, aiming for Grace, but it was a bit of a long shot – literally! – because Grace was surrounded by three Angels defenders, and the ball ran through to the Angels goalie.

The goalie swung her leg back to thump the ball downfield again. I don't know what happened, but she badly mistimed her kick, and instead of the ball flying up into the air, it stayed low. And it was coming straight towards me!

I trapped the ball, brought it down and immediately headed for the Angels penalty area.

'Get up there!' I could hear Georgie yelling. 'Jasmin needs support!'

Suddenly the penalty area seemed full of Angels defenders. I could see Grace, Ruby and Lauren among them, but it looked impossible to pass to any of them. I pushed the ball towards Grace, but a big Angels defender blocked the ball. Lauren pounced on it and tried to set Ruby up for the goal, but yet another Angels defender got the ball away. Grace lunged forward then, and she and the defender battled for control of the ball.

It was becoming a mad goalmouth scramble, and Hannah, Debs and Emily had rushed to join in. If the Angels got the ball away, we'd be left with big holes in defence, I thought anxiously. As the Angels player got the ball away from Grace, I slid in and just got a toe to it. It flew towards the goal...

And hit the post!

'Oh no!' I groaned. But Grace was there to collect the ball as it bounced back into the penalty area. There were three Angels players standing on the line, including the goalie, but somehow Grace managed to poke the ball between two of them.

'GOAL!' I yelled.

The Angels looked utterly shocked. They couldn't believe it, but then, neither could the Stars! One player down against the third-placed team in the league, and we'd somehow managed to score!

'I don't know how we did that,' Grace said with a grin as we celebrated. 'Great stuff!'

'Nice one, Grace!' I said, glowing with confidence as I slapped her on the back. Maybe we could even go on to win this! Georgie certainly seemed to think so – she was jumping around in her goalmouth yelling, 'Go, Stars! Get another!'

We kicked off again, but as there were only a few minutes left in the first half, there was no real time for the Angels to get an attack going. When the whistle blew for half-time, we all rushed over to Ria.

'Girls, I just don't believe it!' she laughed. 'You not only kept a clean sheet, you actually *scored* too!'

'I know, it's mental, isn't it?' Lauren beamed, grabbing a bottle of water.

'I hope we can keep going for the second half,' Hannah added.

'Well, well, well!' Georgie was staring across the pitch. 'Look who's arrived.'

Sienna was running towards us, wearing her

Stars kit. She looked *very* apologetic.

'I'm so sorry, Ria!' she announced. 'We overslept, and then my mum didn't have time to drop me off, so I had to get the bus. Nightmare!'

It might have been true, I suppose. Or it might not.

'Good to see you at last, Sienna,' Ria said coolly. 'You can play the second half. I'll just go and clear it with the ref.'

'Sorry, guys,' Sienna said as Ria went off. 'Oh, and Jasmin, sorry you've got to sit out now I'm here.'

'Oh no, I'm playing any way,' I told her. 'Debs is ill.'

'Really.' Sienna raised her eyebrows. 'Well, that's great. So, come on, what's the score? How many goals have the Angels got?'

'None,' Georgie replied.

Sienna looked very surprised, and, actually, not very pleased. I was more sure than ever now that she'd been late on purpose, just so she could make a drama out of turning up late to save the day. *So* Sienna!

'So it's nil-nil, then,' she remarked.

'No,' Hannah replied. 'Grace scored. We're winning one-nil.'

'No thanks to *you*,' Georgie muttered, glaring at Sienna.

'You're leading one-nil!' Sienna exclaimed. 'With ten players?'

'Absolutely,' Lauren confirmed, a naughty twinkle in her eyes. 'Looks like we don't really need you, doesn't it, Sienna?'

Sienna looked furious as Ria came running back to us.

'Right, all sorted,' she said. 'Now we've got a team of eleven again, we can *really* start to play.'

I was determined to put my feelings about Sienna aside for the good of the team, and I could hear Grace giving Georgie a lecture about doing that very same thing! But somehow, when the second half kicked off, the Stars didn't seem to be playing as well as they'd done in the first half with just the ten of us. Of course, it helped having the extra player just because the numbers were now even. But because all the Stars were wary of Sienna, she didn't seem to add a whole lot to the team apart from being an extra body.

I soon noticed that, as usual, Sienna was keeping the ball to herself far too much. In the first ten minutes we had a great chance to go two up when Sienna took the ball into the Angels penalty area after an admittedly fantastic run. I was standing unmarked with a great chance to score, and I waved, trying to attract her attention. But Sienna completely ignored me and had a shot herself from a narrow angle. The ball went out and hit the side netting.

I thought that maybe Sienna didn't want to pass to *me*, but she did exactly the same thing with Grace and Ruby when they were both in a better position to score. I could see that Ria was getting very annoyed with Sienna, and she was pacing up and down the touchline, rolling her eyes. Georgie wasn't so restrained. I could hear her yelling, *Pass, Sienna!* but Sienna ignored her.

Somehow the Stars hung on. The Angels really *battered* our goal in the last five minutes, but we all went back to help Georgie defend (except Sienna, of course!) and somehow we managed to scramble the ball away every time. We were all getting tired and Sienna was annoying us, but our grit and determination pulled us through. I'd never been so glad to hear the final whistle, though, because I was almost on my knees with exhaustion. YAY! We'd won!

'Guys, you were FABULOUS!' Grace shouted. Panting hard, she flung her arms around me and

Ruby. Poor old Ruby looked like she was ready to collapse, and I wasn't far behind! The others came to join us, and we celebrated with big hugs.

Not Sienna, though. She stood aside, looking rather bored.

'Aren't you celebrating, Sienna?' Georgie asked. That menacing glint was in her eyes again! 'Oh no, I forgot – you didn't *actually* do anything to help us win, did you!'

'Well, to be honest, I think I made a bit of a mistake joining the Stars,' Sienna announced with a yawn. 'I don't really enjoy playing with you lot, so I think I'll join the Blackbridge Belles instead.'

And she strolled off to the changing-room, leaving us standing there with our mouths wide open.

'Well!' Georgie could hardly speak, she was so furious. 'What a cheek that girl's got!'

'The Belles are welcome to her,' Hannah added.

'That is *so* Sienna,' I said. I could even smile about it. I was reasonably confident I could deal with Sienna from now on, both at school and on the football pitch.

Just then Ria came dashing over. She looked incredibly excited.

'Girls, I just got a text about the Belles' game,' she

told us. 'And guess what? They only drew against the Burnlee Bees!'

'*Really?*' Georgie roared with delight. 'That's fantastic!' And she flung herself on Ria and gave her a big hug. I couldn't believe it – and Ria certainly couldn't either! Georgie then turned bright red, looking very sheepish.

'Brilliant!' I gasped. 'So that means we're catching the Belles up! Er – how many points are between us now?' I was simply too excited to work it out!

'It means they're just *one* point ahead of us,' Hannah said. 'We're right on their tail!'

'And after Christmas, we'll overtake them,' Katy added confidently.

'You bet!' Grace laughed.

We slung our arms around each other's shoulders and strolled off the field, chattering away.

I felt *so* happy that this wasn't my last game for the Stars after all, and I was already looking forward to battling away for promotion after Christmas alongside my best friends in the whole world.

Silently I vowed there and then to get the most *gorgeous* Chrissie prezzies I could afford for Grace,

Hannah, Lauren, Katy, Georgie and my gran.

Because without the love and support of Team Jasmin, I wouldn't be looking forward to *anything* except a career as an accountant!

THE BEAUTIFUL GAME

Read on for an extract of the sixth book in the series!

'A sure-fire hit for every girl!'
Faye White, England Women's Captain

THE BEAUTIFUL GAME

Friends and football – the perfect match

KATY'S REAL LIFE

NARINDER DHAMI
Author of the BEND IT LIKE BECKHAM novel

978 1 408 30426 6   £5.99

As the season comes to an end, Katy's torn between her friends, football and her family. Will the real Katy emerge to save the day?

THE BEAUTIFUL GAME

Can't get enough of Jasmin and her friends?

Here's a taster of book 6 –

KATY'S REAL LIFE

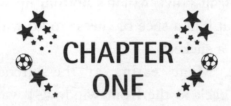

CHAPTER ONE

'Kay-teee! *KAY-TEE!*'

'Milan, be quiet!' I jumped off the window seat and tiptoed into the kitchen past my dad who was asleep on the saggy old sofa. He hadn't been very well again yesterday, which made four nights in a row he hadn't been able to sleep. 'What's the matter *now?*'

My little brother Milan was in our shoebox-sized kitchen (no, really, it IS the size of a shoebox). He beamed up at me. 'I'm hungry, Katy,' he announced.

'What, again?' I said sternly. 'You've had two biscuits already.' The problem is, it's just *sooo* difficult to be stern with Milan because he's incredibly cute! He's only four years old and he has dark hair the same colour as mine, but his is curly and glossy instead of sleek and smooth. I'd kill for those curls! And he also has these huge chocolate-brown eyes that melt me every time. I'm such a sucker.

'No more biscuits,' I said, and gave him an apple from the fruit bowl. Milan's bottom lip wobbled a bit, so I cut him a slice of cheese to go with it. Told you I was a sucker!

Leaving Milan eating at the kitchen table, I hurried back to the front window. I was looking out for my mum who'd gone to her early morning cleaning job. It was a grey, blowy March morning, but I didn't care because it was Saturday and that meant FOOTBALL – one of my favourite things in the whole world. I'd joined the Springhill Stars Under-Thirteens team almost exactly a year ago, and most Saturday mornings during the season I'd sat here worrying that my mum wouldn't get home from work in time for me to make it to the match.

Today we were playing the Pickford Panthers. Mum was a bit later than usual, and I was getting anxious. We only had three games left until the end of the season, and the Stars were in the running for promotion to the next league. But to do that, we had to overtake our biggest rivals, the Blackbridge Belles, because only the top team went through automatically. The next four teams had to go into the play-offs. Scary!

Since we'd narrowed the gap between the Belles and us to one point, just before Christmas, things had been up and down. We'd got knocked out of the County Cup in the third round, and we'd lost a league game here and there. To our dismay, we'd dropped back to three points behind the Belles by the end of January. But then we'd pulled ourselves together a bit and the Belles had had a bad spell, which meant the gap was now one point again.

'Can I have some more cheese, Katy?' Milan called from the kitchen. I jumped up and went in to him again.

'No,' I whispered, putting my finger to my lips. 'And don't wake Dad up.'

It wasn't just Saturdays, either, when I had to be at home. My mum worked every day of the week except Sundays, and someone had to be around to watch Milan because my dad wasn't always well enough to do it. Mum worked so hard, she didn't always have time to do the shopping and cooking and cleaning, so I helped out with that, too. I had to juggle things like crazy – housework and homework and school and matches and training twice a week and seeing my friends. I was *always* clock-watching.

I know that Jasmin, Georgie, Grace, Hannah and Lauren think there's something mysterious about me. I was having a pretty stressful time a month or two ago when Dad was quite ill, and after training one day, I was outside the changing-room door while the others were inside. I heard Jasmin say 'Look, why don't we just *ask* her what's going on? It's totally obvious that something's not right, and we might be able to help.'

I guessed instantly that the girls were talking about me.

'You know what Katy's like,' Georgie had said. 'She doesn't tell us *anything* about her home life.'

'If we asked, I'd feel like we were sticking our noses in.' That was Lauren. 'We ought to wait until Katy tells us herself – *if* she wants to.'

I went into the changing-room then, and the girls stopped talking about me and started discussing the match that coming Saturday instead. I was relieved, but I also felt a bit upset that they *hadn't* questioned me about what was wrong. I didn't want them to, really, because I admit that I *do* get a bit prickly and embarrassed sometimes when I'm asked things I don't want to answer. But this time I sort of hoped they *would*. Do you understand that? Because I don't!

Anyway, whatever the girls think, there's nothing very mysterious about my real life...

Dad, Mum, Milan and me came to England from Poland just over three years ago. We used to live in a little village about fifty kilometres south of Warsaw (which is the capital city of Poland, if you didn't know!). My grandparents still live there, and we had to leave our little dog, Max, with them, which upset me a lot. My gran writes every week and tells us how Max is doing.

At first, everything in England was fine. We came to Melfield because some of my Mum and Dad's friends from Poland were already here, and my dad found work straightaway. He's a carpenter, and he made all our furniture back home. I could already speak English quite well because we were studying it at school. My dad speaks English brilliantly – he'd visited England a few times before and he likes watching English and American films. Dad often spoke English to me and Milan at home because he wanted us to be good at different languages. My mum didn't like it that much because she only speaks Polish. Anyway, I'm glad Dad *did* help me improve my English because when we moved here, it didn't really take me long to fit in.

Lots of things are different here to Poland, though, and it took me *so* long to get used to them! Everyone thinks Poland is really cold in winter, and it is, but England feels so much colder. My dad says it's because it's so damp and wet here. In Poland the snow makes everything look really pretty, and people are ready for it, so everything goes on mostly as normal. Here in England, everything seems to stop for snow!

There are *so* many more people in England, too. I looked up *Warsaw* and *London* on the internet in the library, and Warsaw has about 1.7 million people while London has eight million. EIGHT MILLION – it's amazing, isn't it? My dad took us to London once on a sight-seeing trip before he got ill, and I think most of those eight million people were there in Trafalgar Square at the same time as us!

About the Author

Narinder Dhami lives in Cambridge with her husband Robert and their three cats, but was originally born in Wolverhampton. Her dad came over from India in 1954, and met and married her mum, who is English. Narinder always wanted to write, but after university taught in London for ten years before becoming a writer.

For the last thirteen years Narinder has been a full-time author. She has written over 100 children's books, as well as many short stories and articles for children's magazines. *Team Jasmin* is the fifth book in The Beautiful Game series.

Since her childhood, Narinder has been a huge football fan.

A message from the England Women's Captain
FAYE WHITE

With over 1.5 million playing the game, girls' and women's football is now the number one female sport. I have played for Arsenal and England ladies since I was sixteen. I grew up kicking a ball around – in the playground, at school, or in my back garden. I was the only girl playing amongst boys, but I never let that stop me, and I joined my first club at thirteen.

For me, playing football has always been about passion and enjoyment. It's a great way to challenge myself, be active, gain self-confidence, and learn about teamwork.

I have gone on to captain and play for England seventy times, and achieved my dream of playing in a World Cup (China 2007). I've won over twenty-five honours for Arsenal, including the treble, and the Women's UEFA Cup.

Do you love football as much as me?

Then maybe, just maybe, you can follow in my shoes...
Practice, be passionate and strive for your dream. Enjoy!

Find out more about Faye and girls' football at...

www.faye-white.co.uk   www.thefa.com/womens
www.arsenal.com/ladies   www.fairgamemagazine.co.uk